Footprints of Childhood in the Dust

Books by Dr. Chandrakant Sheth

Poetry—Pavan Ruperi; Ughadati Divalo; Gagan Kholti Bari; Praudhshikshan Gitmala; Gagan Kholti Baari; Saksharta Gito; Shage Ek Jhalahalie; Ek Tahuko Pand Ma; Undaan Mathee Aave, Unchaan Ma Lai Jaay; Jal Vadal Ne Vij; Gagan Dharaa Par Tadkaa Niche; Had Ma Anhad; Shabd Ma Maun, Maun Ma Shabd; etc.

Essays—Nand Samvedi; Anandparv; Chahera Bhitar Chahera; Vaninu Sat, Vanini Shakti; Akhand Diva; Rudi Janso Jeevtarnee; Dive Dive Dev; etc.

Satire—Het Ane Halvaash; Vahaal Ane Vinod; Kankarichaalo Ne Paththarmaaro and Halvi Kalam Na Phool. E Balkaniwaali Chhokri Ane..., E Ane Hu. Kaavyapratyaksh, Arthaantar, Kaant, Umashankar Joshi: Jhalak Ane Zankhi, Sahitya:

Criticism—Praan Ane Pravartana, Sahitya: Tej Ane Taasir, Swaminarayan Santkavita: Aaswad Ane Avbodh, Gujarati Ma Viraamchinnho, Bhaktkavi Shri Narsinh Mehta: Bhaktikavita Nu Saatatya Ane Siddhi, Ayraninu Swaroop Ane Eno Sahitya Ma Viniyog, etc.

Children's books—Anil no Chabutro, Ghode Chadi Ne Avu Chhu..., Hu To Chalu Mari Jem!, Zaanjharbhaine Jadya Pag..., Kidibaie Naat Jamaadi!, Chaandaliyani Gadi, etc.

Eminent Awards

Kumar Chandrak, Narmad Suvarna Chandrak, Ranjitram Suvarna Chandrak, Uma-Snehrashmi Prize, Dhanji Kanji Gandhi Suvarna Chandrak, Narsinh Mehta Award, and Sahitya Gaurav Puraskar etc.

Footprints of Childhood in the Dust

Written originally in Gujarati by

Chandrakant Sheth

Published by
PRABHAT PRAKASHAN PVT. LTD.
4/19 Asaf Ali Road,
New Delhi-110 002 (INDIA)
e-mail: prabhatbooks@gmail.com

ISBN 978-93-5562-168-9
Footprints of Childhood in the Dust
by Shri Chandrakant Sheth

Edition
First, 2024

Price
₹ 400.00 (Rupees Four Hundred only)

Translated into English by
Dr. Kalki Krishna

Printed at
R-Tech Offset Printers, Delhi

In Front of and Behind the Footprints

In my forty-sixth year of age, I felt: Come on, let's meet that little Chandrakant of mine. Have to go there again, where I have come from. Have to walk on that bumpy and dusty track. The feet which have become accustomed to walking on the bitumen-path may or may not like it, but there is pleasure even in walking—and in that too, walking backwards is special. From a distance, not only the mountains, but also the time passed seems beautiful. I had to see by bringing out, through the alchemy of memory and imagination, those footprints that were buried in the dust of childhood and adolescence of the past. By understanding the script of those marks, I had to enjoy the emotions that arise from understanding them. Reliving what has been lived, living it in a more interesting way has been an undertaking here. These marks are the result of that very taste-targeted undertaking.

I thought I only had to see my own footprints. But as I kept looking at the footprints, I realised that these footprints were as mysterious as a maze. They can also lead me astray. In each mark, the image of many marks is seen mixed. Traces of elders, friends, neutrals, opponents—all emerge simultaneously. There are many unfamiliar marks in it too, but if I speak from my heart, what was unfamiliar at that time is not unfamiliar now, what seemed to be an opponent is no longer an opponent now.

I feel the vibration of immense compassion of the Supreme Being in my being. Earth, water, air, sky—all these are truly extremely compassionate and illusive; they allowed me to walk. I could walk—could take a few steps here and there—could make marks. It is good that in these the footprints are found not only of my relatives or human relatives, but also of animals and birds.

What kind of stories with tinkling flavours—are sparked by these marks. There is a little sipping of these stories here.

Questions arise in my mind again and again: Who drives us and why do we move? Why would it have been said *'charan vai madhu vindati dand'* (the stick finds honey while walking)? Even to know this, one will have to walk. There is something that can be understood only by walking. The secret of gait can be caught while walking. Their identity can be obtained only from the footprints—true and certain.

The one who made these marks is a Gamadiya, a boy roaming around wearing lunar-and-solar patched tights and a ruffled vest. His name—Bachuro-Chandrio-Chandro, and the one trying to identify him is the poet 'Chandurio': that is Dr. Chandrakant Sheth—a servant (professor) of the Gujarat Vidyapeeth, and the Director-Professor of 'K.L. Swadhyaya Mandir' run by the Gujarati Sahitya Parishad. There is a considerable difference between the two. The tricks-and-tactics of worldly affairs directly hinder many things. Still, there is a bridge between the two. The poet, the creator of 'Chanduria', believes that the friendship of that 'Chanduria' is not worth losing. That is why, with the idea of cementing this friendship, one feels happy by illuminating such scars through words. Due to the zeal to include everyone in this happiness, this book has been published.

These footprints are mine; this is just an incident or reason. Everyone has a right on these marks. I am definitely present in these marks, but 'I' is not the ego, but like a pole-position which is essential for the creator's action. Manhar Bhai (Poet Manhar Modi) became the instrument to bring out the *Nand Samvedi* (collection of fine essays) in me to the form of words. I am also indebted to him for putting these marks into words.

It is hoped that a special and creative encounter be occurred to everyone with the *'pranpurush' (*soul-person*)* in their own way which has been expressed in these marks. Even if this work becomes an instrument in such an interview, it is sufficient. There is nothing left except expressing gratitude from my side.

This work was published in serial form in *'Udgaar'* and *'Samakaleen',* many friends had praised it then. Naming them all would result in a long list, so I am postponing it, but I express my gratitude to all of them. Their encouragement gave me the courage and strength to search for these 'marks', how can I forget this? Here I fondly remember my friend-and-publisher Bhagatbhai and Saurabhbhai of *'Samakaleen',* who helped in achieving the love of a large audience. In the future, I wish that I obtain the love and affection of you all and avail of your help in filling the gaps within me.

21 July, 1984 **—Chandrakant Sheth**

In the Light of Memory...*

Honourable Mr. President, Noble Ladies and Gentlemen, First of all, I express my happiness that *Dhoolmani Paglio* (Footprints on the Dust) has been awarded the Sahitya Akademi award—I express my gratitude to all those who have been instrumental in this.

On this occasion, if I request you some things in the context of 'Footprint on the Dust', I hope you will appreciate those.

'Footprints on the Dust' is the story of my childhood and adolescence. If I can write more truthfully and effectively, I can write only about myself. Naturally, there may also be some specificity in this due to my personal context. I should present such thing from my life, which I find more-and-more flavoursome. That thing belonged to my childhood and adolescence only. There was no pollution like today. There was no such load or tension on the mind like today. Life then was a game, a play. At that time, one could comfortably talk to the wall, I had enough time to glance after the ant. Then, one's clothes could be easily taken off in the rain. Without compunction or hesitation, the jujubes from Gauri's palm could be taken with such privilege as though those were all for myself. To remember that

* Speech given at the time of receiving the Sahitya Akademi Award.

time, to live while remembering it, I used to feel like using revitalizing-ambrosia (*amrit sanjivani*). So much remains safe inside. So much remains alive in itself. As I kept recognising the footprints of my childhood and teenage years in the light of memory, a piece of life full of divinatory-play (*leela*) kept becoming revealed from each footprint. I have been touching the ambrosial vastness of my inner world in every trace. What I used to think of as left and lost was flavour fully present in me by spreading its roots. Apart from the practical calculations of worldliness, apart from prejudiced rules and prohibitions, such an absolutely taste-worthy world was swinging inside me like a sweet fruit. When I picked up the pen to write about my childhood, that world made me drenched with the flavour of divinatory-play. Those who had done a break-up with me in my childhood were also calling me with great affection. All those who stayed away from me at that time for some inexplicable reason shadowed me with the rights of acceptance. I began to feel the child of my aspirations, the dream child, alive and playing inside me in a way full of divine play. I didn't realise when that boy established his complete authority over me; it was if I've become his toy. My compunction and hesitation disappeared. The plank of my age came down. I was transformed like Yayati. Becoming a child again by an Anasuya-like power, I started tasting my childhood like a jujube. I reunited with my childhood friends. I started trying to weave my childhood into words, to make it real. With a creative passion, I was trying to match the cadence of my footprints with the words and that is why in front of those words—as if those were my childhood friends—in that way I started warmly opening my heart. That's how I got into the game.

This work is the story of this very game. Then the city's coal-tar road did not touch the heel of my feet. The thrill of innovatively making footprints in the granular-porridge-like dust used to push me by twisting-and-turning to have a conference with stone and water by lifting me from my harsh present. I had organised the conference with full flavouring-interest. All of you listened to it with affection and patience. While hearing about that conference, you became a resident of my inner world. This increased my world of affection and joy and filled my heart with a sense of gratitude. Word that not only became an emotion-bridge taking me by lifting from the present to the past, carrying me towards infancy from maturity, getting me arrived at the fair from solitude, connecting me the alone to the many, but also it thus became an indication of divinatory-play, which put me in cognition of remembrance about the real engagement with affection and truth, beauty and eternity. The word itself has enriched my life by giving me a vision of your affinity towards me.

Today I salute this Word-the-Almighty (*Shabd-Brahm*) and all of you. May the music of the loving-company of ours become more-and-more effective and do honourably establish us in an indescribable super-consciousness—with such auspicious desire.

09 February, 1987 **—Chandrakant Sheth**

Translator's Note

While entrusting any translation-work to the readers, it has been customary to furnish such disclosures to clearly indicate the linguistic treatments adopted by the translator while translating the original text in order to maintain, as per the global norms set for translating a literary work, not even an iota of compromise with the literary characteristics including expression, style and overall impact inherent in the original text so that when its translated version is presented to a wide readership in one more language, even at that time, the same spontaneity and soil-smell should also be retained everywhere on its pages as they were in the original text. This note is nothing but a compliance with that very custom. But before following that custom, I would like to write briefly about the significance of this original Gujarati book and its dignified author for those—especially English readers—who may not be familiar with contemporary Gujarati literature.

This book–now in your hands–is an English translation of the highly sought after book *Dhoolmani Paglio* written by Chandrakant Sheth, an eminent Gujarati litterateur of our time. Apart from being much-discussed and widely applauded, this book was also awarded the Best Gujarati Book Award in 1986 by India's Central 'Sahitya Akademi'.

Apart from being a milestone book in Gujarati literature, *Dhoolmani Paglio* is significant because of having a bouquet of the flowers of emotion ,of different colours and shades. Although it is a collection of autobiographical memoirs where the author is in a retrospective mood to look at his childhood past from the turret of the present, it is neither an autobiography as such nor the memoir in the prevalent sense, but forms a confluence of both the streams. The author, Chandrakant Sheth has been known for wearing many hats—he is an excellent poet, prolific essayist, able critic, writer of children's literature, deep-rooted in the soil, erudite expert in Indian-ness, a keen observer, visionary creator, enlightened person. The glimpse of every feather of his various hats can be found in *Dhoolmani Paglio,* just like one tests a single grain of rice taking out of a boiling pot in order to check whether the entire rice is well-cooked or not. Using the words of Chandrakant Topiwala, a famous Gujarati litterateur honoured with Sahitya Akademi Award, it can rightly be said that *Dhoolmani Paglio* is a 'catalogue of sensitive prose' where each-and-every emotion of human being can be seen written at one place. Be it his poems collected in *Ughadati Diwalo,* his children's rhymes collected in *Hoo To Chaloo Mari Jem,* his ghazals collected in *Ek Tahuko Pandma,* his essays of light-humour collected in *Vahal Ane Vinod,* his modernist essays collected in *Nand Samvedi,* or his erudition of the Vedas and Upanishads shown in essays collected in *Vaninu Sat, Vanini Shakti* and through different discourses—the glimpse and dignity of all these can clearly be seen on the pages of *Dhoolmani Paglio* just like the details of a night-jasmine are become visible in the torchlight. It is always best to read the entire literature composed by Chandrakant Sheth, but if for any reason this is not possible then it is said that reading only this book—

Dhoolmani Paglio—would be enough for going through and tasting his writing art.

Translating such an excellent book into English has been very challenging. The entire text of this book is written in a poetic manner. Due to this quality, not only various emotion-gems that are visible layer after layer there at different places, but the resonance of each of those is also heard beyond the words. For a philosopher-turned-filmmaker like me, who by the nature of his work-is bound to observe the hidden more than the apparent, it was not possible to go in a nonchalant way ignoring those. All such gems can be traced glittering in this translation, too, as in original text—though being moulded in the nature of English. Sentences, written in talking mode, vary in length—right from containing just a single word to those covering almost half-page space in the original text. No matter how long the sentences are, whether simple or compound, those have been translated in the same way. If the original text describes something in a single sentence, then why can it not be translated into English in a single sentence as well—this has also been challenging. But it has been successfully executed everywhere, because without it, the flavour of the original text would not have been captured in its translated version and all the impact would have been ruined.

This work of translation is the *translation* of the original text in exact sense. The translation of this book could also be done by substituting words or sentences from the original language into English, but then the result wouldn't qualify even to be considered a sub-standard translation, it would be mechanical; this could also be done by rewriting the original-language content into English, but then it would has been as if it was written by me, instead of a translation work. It would ultimately be my own writing containing all the shades of my own style; this could also be done by transcribing expressions from the original text into English, but then it would be paraphrasing where the essence of the original text is completely missed. Rejecting these three methods, in order to make it a translation in the real sense, a challenging method has been implemented here, which is at present universally practiced while translating a literary work. It has rendered this translation work as *not a mere translation,* but as if the author himself is writing this book in English with his style of writing and full range of his skills. Needless to say, the original book has been translated taking into account the outlook that the translated version must look like the original writing of author's own rather than a translated work.

At many places in the original book, the words derived from completely Indian concepts—like: *shabd-brahm, naad-brahm, leela, pragy, yaksh-prashn, ida, pingla, sushumna,* etc.—have been used, which cannot be translated into one word in any non-Indian language of the world. Along with writing such words in their original form in Roman script, their purport has also been briefly explained in English in the running text itself. Similarly, very often the author has coined composite words—like: *brahmanand-sahodar-anand, sancharini-deepshikha, snehopanishad, navaras-ruchirahyadaikamayi-srishti, manahkalp,* etc.—using Indian soil; the purport of all of those has also been briefly explained in English in the running text, besides being given in the Roman script. Also, some new footnotes have been added to clarify the relevant content.

As one of the most translated Nobel laureates José de Sousa Saramago once said—every great writer has an unparallel style of writing, so the best way to translate their work is to maintain their style even in the translated version. No doubt, Chandrakant Sheth has also an unparalleled style of writing—and, here, I would humbly like to dare in writing that his writing style has been maintained to the maximum possible extent in this translation work. I don't know him personally, have never met him—yet I would like to thank him for his excellent book, *Dhoolmani Paglio,* let me become acquainted with such a unique writing style.

09 December, 2023

—Dr. Kalki Krishna
Mumbai–400049

1

This morning I was looking at a magazine. It had photographs of a person of different ages. I loved seeing those photographs. The face of childhood and the face of old age. I started searching for the similarities and differences between these two faces, how the face changes with age. But is it easy to interview this secret? Can the mystery of time be captured without tasting time? And how to perceieve the taste of time?

I sat down to open myself once again. I took out one form after another from my life-box. I had no idea that my box would be so magical. Different things kept coming out one after the other. In the end, the place has come where the memory gets tired and stops. Okay, I thought. From here I start the affectionate talking with time. I will have a conversation with my time, with myself. I will say what I have felt; I will also say the feeling I am having today and also the feeling I had then. My aim is to make the time speak through myself, to open the life-box in front of me. Let see at least, what is safe in this? Why is it safe?

In the year 1938, Halol village of Panchmahal district, which is also a subdivision; I can see its face completely blurred. Appears wrapped around the womb. I try to bring its memory in my reach by pulling it, but I fail. As if many small and big heaps of darkness are visible. I must have appeared from one such heap. My elders say, "There was an earthquake after your birth, when you were in the cradle. Everyone went out except you...even the mother! Then suddenly remembered and took you out of the house." It's correct. Even today many 'quakes' happen under my feet, but the ones who can get me out are as though missing.

I could not get anything from the shaken earth of Halol. In just one photograph, I see my infant form in the mother's lap. With the skill of whose hands today's form emerged out of that, it is a matter of our prying. Leaving Halol, now we have to reach Dahod.

Dahod and Bhil have become one by mixing in me. Black body, black dress and silver earrings, bare feet, bracelet in hand, bow and arrow must be there. Usually a nappy, but a white cloth wrapped for the respect of the colony, a piece of white cloth trying to keep the dry hair flying on the head in discipline. Whenever I see such a Bhil disguise, I see the raised current of Dahod's watery earth in it. If there is hardness in the land of Dahod, then it has equally the sweetness of raw maize. Along with hard work, there is glee of the indigenous-people in it. The mountains and the forest have mingled with each other. Stone and water have been constantly penetrating each other. Like removing the leaves and fibres of the maize cob, I remove the layers of time one after the other. Like the shine of milky maize grains, a charming child-form of Dahod is emerging in front of my eyes today. There is play of prying in his eyes, the taste of affection on his face and the light of devoutness. As if time marked in the dust is matching its steps with the dance-art of the crows. The tinkling of anklet-bells of the Hori singers and the strumming of cymbals of the water-carrying-women are heard together. By shutting my eyes, I surrender myself to a mountain stream and see myself sitting on a sackcloth bed at the end of a locality in the sweet winter morning sun.

I don't remember my dress clearly. Must have worn a *fatuhi* made of cotton. Nearby, father is wearing a peacock-coloured *fatuhi*. There is a turban of red scarf on his head. He has a rosary and a book on the routine of Vaishnavism. Two or four boys from the locality have arrived. Father gets them sung while clapping in his loud voice:

"Radheshyam kaho, Sitaram kaho,
Is nam ke bina beda par na ho."
(Say Radheshyam, say Sitaram,
No ship sails without this name.)

All of us boys would sing this tune loudly by pulling the veins of our throats and clap. The cold of the winter morning does not touch us even after being close to us. We are engrossed in watching the steam coming out of our mouths and in singing tunes, while *pak*-pieces come there. Our Radheshyam has to wait for some time. The pieces of *pak* get warmed in the throat that immediately Radheshyam stands up again as a refrain-line. Our tune starts again. 'Say Radheshyam...!'

At that time, the movie which used to play in front of our eyes, the group of water-carrying women along with cowherds would be special there. How the lovely Gomati cow of Chhagan, who gives milk at our place, goes on swinging the frill of her neck and jingling bells! And those water-carrying women! I can probably see them better today than they did to me then. Narmada aunty—having a volumetric physique, impressive, completely devoted to God. Avoiding everyone, she used to walk far and wide but with energy. Radha Ramturi used to go along with her. Very mischievous, kept laughing and would be making catena as if made of pearls. As if the playful fishes of the pond do not shine in her eyes. And that Sharduri. Even if I didn't speak, she would certainly get me speak by tickling. And that Revali, who had just got married. She did not leave my father in mischief by taking on her long veil. While getting her soft eyes danced, blossoming red roses on her cheeks, she bowing slightly said to my father, "Devotee uncle, you have made a good gathering, haven't you...! You have included this boy also in the psalm-singing!"

"It is good thing!"

"It's absolutely right, make the whole village a devotee's village."

"If God wills, it too will happen."

Later, Revali would go away while laughing and priding. Sometimes, in case she has brought a wood-apple or something like that, she would stop and leave it on our sacks. There was a unique flexibility in the gait of that Revali. Even without the anklet, the path would have been tinkling with her, I guess today. Her group of friends was large and our devotee group used to get the benefit of their sweet-sour bickering and jokes every day.

At that time the importance of the village pond was more than the Olympic ground for us. A huge banyan tree on the bank of the pond. Bechat, the son of a peon and our brother, was a great swimmer. Climbing fast on the banyan tree, reaching the very top, he would jump into the pond. A big bounce of water with a splashing sound. Going to the bottom of the water, Bechat would come out of it in the blink of eye. This Bechat was as glorious for me as Thakurji of the temple. I would roam around behind him. I would pick up the words coming out of his mouth and he would also very generously distribute pieces of *kamalgatta* (lotus-seed) to all of us as an offering of his bravery. If Bechat wanted to smoke *beedi,* I would find a burning dry-dung for him from anywhere. If he felt thirsty, three or four disciples would run home together to get water and in return he would take care of us. He used to take full care of our wellbeing.

In the evening, when we would go to Shankarji's

temple, there would be a lot of brawling about who should play the drum and bell during the *aarti.* At such times, our leader Bechat would come marching forward proudly. As soon as he arrived, all the boys who wanted to play drums and bells would divide into two groups in his honour. Bechat would look around, everyone would try to attract his kind glance. Sometimes, it would be my turn. Bechat would hold me by the waist and make me sit in front of the drum; then there would be me and the drum. We all would make joint efforts to make the *aarti* event as grand as possible. Those who did not get chance to play drums or bells at least had their hands to clap. They would make the joy explode by clapping enthusiastically and then enjoy it.

In the light of this *aarti*-event, it seemed as if the entire village had assumed a different form. The usual noise of the entire village gets drowned in the sweet sound of *aarti's* bell. A golden line of spirituality would be visible above the blackish dustiness. How beautiful the whiteness of the raw coconut *prasad* (offerings) looked in the miniature palms in the evening. I was very fond of the beauty of the *aarti* performed by the temple priest. I was fascinated by the way he would give delicate twists the *aarti* by fixing it at a height of space, and I was equally fascinated by Bechat's art of cleverly distributing the offerings.

The distribution of the offerings used to take place in the way he wanted. Sometimes I would myself ask Bechat to distribute the offerings and then Bechat would mostly hand over the responsibility to me. I used to distribute the offerings to all the kings and paupers in a socialist manner after reserving a good portion of the offerings for Bechat.

It seemed as if the entire village used to swing with us in the rhythm of this *aarti*. It seemed as if everyone's tiredness of the day would have gone away after *aarti.* Everyone would sit here and there in the hall of the temple, boasting and playing all kinds of games. Due to fear of my father, I would reach home early, but then it seemed as if only the body had reached home, the mind was still circling around the *aarti* of the temple like a moth.

□

My father was a Pushtimargi Vaishnav. Worship of Thakurji at home used to be performed with full pomp and show. There was a similar atmosphere of devotion in the temple and home. Thakurji would have been there in our games, too. I remember an incident about *hindola* (carousel). In my father's absence, my elder brother took off the *dhoti* from the peg and wore it as best he could. After that, he also took off *saree* and *lehenga* from the peg and decorated the *hindola* with those. Decorated towards *jhular* with *lehenga* and *hindola* with *saree* at the back. Planted photos etc., onto the *hindola* after taking those off the wall and. At that moment, he got some idea and told me by calling, "You have to enact as Thakurji and sit on the *hindola*." I was completely aware of the manner of sitting on my elder brother's carousel. I therefore, refused for fear of falling. If he had his way, he would certainly have got me sitting on the carousel, but he was afraid that in case I started crying, the entire game would be disrupted, so he released me from his custody. But then he caught hold of sister and said, "You have to move the carousel as Jashoda." The sister said, "Go, go, why should I play role as Jashoda? I will swing as Thakurji, you will swing me as Mukhiyaji." This delightful idea appealed more to the elder brother. He said, "It is not right that you become Thakurji. Girls cannot become Thakurji. I will become one." He taking a toy flute sat on the carousel. But the passion for Satyagraha was deep inside the sister. She didn't even swing the carousel. The elder brother was playing role as Thakurji, how could he swing him by himself? There was a lot of tussle. The elder brother got excited and the inevitable result of discord came what was to come. The clouds of sister's cry started raining and as a result, the elder brother playing role as Thakurji had to taste the punishment of his father who suddenly arrived there. I remember, that day the father praised my humble attempt to play peacefully.

□

I got many toys in my childhood; among them I had a special bias towards Lalji Maharaj. Many attempts have been made to make Lalji wear the loincloth, but I don't remember obtaining much success. I remember that when it came to placing offerings in front of this Lalji Maharaj, at that time I protested fiercely by weeping in front of my sister. But after many experiences, I realised that whatever is kept in front of Lalji Maharaj is returned in the same form without any reduction, then my enthusiasm to place regular offerings in front of him increased. This Lalji Maharaj does not even eat the *laddu* of his own hand. I remember that once it seemed very inefficient to me and I made a brutal effort to bend that arm. It was good that elder brother arrived on time and Lalji Maharaj's hand with *laddu* remained safe.

This Lalji Maharaj was my staunch companion. He must have heard many of my talks. If he had anything to say, that too I would have said. He had to take bath only when I bathed him and then had to sleep when I put him to sleep. Apart from this Lalji Maharaj, others too were my friends. There was a parrot, a train and also a pair of *gop-gopi*. And the wall was my best friend. Even today that wall is there, but now it bears witness to my silent pain. But I have lost the skill of talking to it. The parrot has long since fled from my toy durbar. The train has also departed, leaving me here in desolate state, writhing in agony like a deserted station.

There is no one here even to say whether another train will come or not. That imposing ride of Dussehra is long gone, and only its traces imprinted in the dust are left. On the basis of these marks, will I be able to bring back the passengers who had gone here?

Today I like this dust very much. In some caste ceremony, it is as if I am putting my hand in a coppersmith's hot pot drenched with *ghee-misri* (clarified butter and sugar-candy), likewise I put my hand in this dust. There is a touch of sweetness on the hand and the mind feels its taste. Just as a stream of *ghee* oozes out from porridge, similarly the mind becomes anxious to escape from someone's sight.

□

2

An experience is remembered again and again. As evening approached, darkness began to set in, the distant horizon became hazy, and then I would, with wide eyes, try to distinguish and resolve the lines of the face of the universe behind the rays of darkness that were getting deeper. While doing this, I also used to have to take the help of memory and imagination. Memory gave light to the vision and imagination helped it to connect with everything. When I try to peep into the past, I experience something similar. To peep into the past, I find it necessary to dig deep into my soil layer by layer. Many such sheets of time are covered one after the other on my childhood creation. I will have to remove them all. Some sheets are so beautiful that when I see them, I forget to remove them for a moment, but my interest is not in the sheet, but in the face of the childhood covered under the sheet. Its bright eyes, its easy humor, its mischievousness—it has an abstruse and deep attraction for me.

This is my world of Dahod. In the dim rainy light of memory, a path becomes visible. The *taziya* procession has started with the echo of 'Ya Hussain'. Ahead is a sixteen-year-old boy wearing a tiger mask, his entire body yellow due to turmeric paste. He pounces like a tiger, takes out his eyes from his mask and moves around jumping from here to there with his claws out; along with this, the noise of drums and dancing is going on there. I am standing near my sister on the platform. My eyes are nowhere else but on that boy wearing the tiger-face. As if I were a goat, he jumps towards me and I start screaming and crying. The tiger takes me by surprise and laughs and tries to silence me by removing the mask. The rest of the scene of *taziya* is seen drowning and rising in tears. I think the shock that I felt on seeing the tiger-face boy laughing like me was different and greater than the shock that I felt on seeing him.

How many memories are woven with these *taziyas*! Out of the five or seven *taziyas* that came out in the village, which faction's *taziya* was the best became a matter of great pride for me when I gained some understanding. Whenever our faction's Muslim brothers would start making *taziya*, I would get deployed to help them. I also used to help in small tasks like fixing the *taziya* foil and applying lace to it. I used to give eye-witnessed reports to everyone about what progress was made in *taziyas* every day. A Muslim peon in my father's office was a master in the art of making *taziyas*. Ever since I came to know this, my respect for him had increased. He seemed to me as glorious as the Chaudhary of my village. When that peon would sit down to make a *taziya*, I would get the privilege of sitting near him because I was the son of his superior. I myself used to play the game of making small *taziyas* by collecting different types of papers at home. I remember that many times, before the *taziyas* of Muharram, we would roam around in the locality carrying such imitated *taziays* and some of our more enthusiastic friends would even experiment with blowing *hool* while dancing, shouting 'Ya Hussain'. At the time of these celebrations, we used whatever came to hand as musical-instruments. If there was a box of straw lying in any warehouse, we making a drum out of it would have got people spellbound. When the childish-ride of our unauthorized *taziya* reached near Vaishnav Haveli in Chaupal, making everyone around laugh, its pride used to increase a bit more. While playing our drums, friends used to go round and round, and beat their hands on the chest in such a way as to make a sound and make loud sounds of 'Ya Hussain'. These loud sounds would have greatly disturbed my father while he was performing *kirtan* in the mansion *(haveli)*. Leaving the *kirtan* he would come to the platform of the mansion and scold all of us, especially me. As a result, our *taziya* procession used to disintegrate reluctantly. I would have had to hear a lot from my childhood friends for this grave-most sin of my father, but due to the weakness of my body and mind, the only solution left for me was to continue making cultured the instinct of pure nonviolence.

The next memory after this is of Vaidya Kaka living behind us. Vaidya Kaka's body was just a skeleton of bones. Seeing him one would assume that this man must have been cursed by Lord Dhanvantari, the founder of Ayurveda. Fushed cheeks, prematurely grey hair, in case his body is exposed one would feel like counting his ribs even though not wanting to do so. But this Vaidya Kaka was a diadem in checking the pulse. My slimness bothered him more than his own slimness. Once he made a complete program of decoction *(kwath)* for a month for me. As soon as the morning dawns, the strong smell of boiling decoction takes away the colour of my pleasant morning. Did I belong to the group of Mirabai who considered poison to be nectar? As soon as the bowl of decoction appeared in front of me, I used to feel like a follower of Satyagraha. Teeth would grind, lips would part and along with clenching of hands, eyes would also squint. Not a single part of the body—even the breath—was ready to accept the decoction; but my Satyagraha had no value for my mother or Vaidyaraj. Those people would reach to apply every trick—praise, price, penalty *(saam, daam, dand)*. Generally, in such cases only the tactics of punishment are successful. All my nerves and organs used to get opened reluctantly. Like, this bitter liquid is poured into the mouth of a bull by inserting a wooden tube. My every pore used to be filled with bitterness. It would have been vocal in the form of a bitter cry, yet my situation was no better than that 'Bhomiya' the not-wandering poet. *"Veraya bol, mara felaya abhaman. Eklo atulo jhankho padyo"* (My words have scattered in the sky. I am left alone and sad). Since my crying had become a daily routine, the fun of persuading-and-coaxing had become rare. I had to silence myself. This month of drinking decoction was very bitter and tear-moistened. I myself wonder why no Hitler emerged in me as a direct response to the extreme atrocities of this decoction.

This Vaidya Kaka used to seem bitter like decoction, but sometimes even sweet like honey. I had an intuitive understanding of what time to go to his place. He would get free time from his Rajwadi Vaishnavi service till one o'clock. At this very moment I would have entered his house. As soon as he saw me, he would shine his teeth which had turned brown with betel leaves and would laugh at me and say, "*Prasadiya Bhagat* (the devotee asking offerings) has arrived?" And I too used to take as much *prasad* as he lovingly gave me and along with having taken that much for this occurring I used to tie some more for the next.

For this Vaidya Kaka, Thakurji was as real as for me. He would offer *bundi laddus, thor, gooja, jalebi, barfi* of gram-flour, etc., to Thakurji. Sometimes, due to excess of devotion, even tasty powder would be offered to Thakurji so that He would not catch indigestion. Today, remembering this fact makes me smile. Would he not have given Thakurji the same bowl of decoction or castor-oil that mother had given me? Perhaps Hari's pulse may be in his hands! Vaidya Kaka was very emotional. He used to become emotional in front of Thakurji. He had died long ago, that too while serving Thakurji.

Today, upon straining my memory, I remember watching the first film of my life 'Sant Dnyaneshwar' in Dahod. It seemed as if a rectangular window opened on the curtain of darkness and characters started coming through that path, one after another. There came a gruesome scene, perhaps of some violent creature. I remember filling the theatre with tears as soon as I heard his roar. After this film, I did not go to the theatre and watch any movie for years. The only exceptions are films shown by the information department of the government. The day the government information department's motor vehicle showing film came to the village, we would keep following it the entire day. Wherever the motor was parked, we would gather in a crowd and inspect it closely from all sides. If ever we got a chance, we wouldn't even let go of the pleasure of touching it. When the motor door was half-open, we would try our best to see what was inside. We always used to think about how the images and sounds of moving humans appeared in this motorised cinema machine. Due to the cinema curtain being kept open, many times we used to sit on both sides of it and watch the film. Whether watching it like this made any difference or not, we would investigate it with scientific seriousness and comparative analysis method. To ensure that those who brought us these government films were happy, and that they exhibited the films at the right time and for a longer period of time, we used to take all the domestic measures to keep them happy: we were always ready to give them cold water from a black earthen pot in a well-cleaned glass. Our humble effort were also to sometimes arrange for tea and snacks for them. Among my companions there were three-four Patels and some elder boys of Baraiya (a caste). They used to remain active in fulfilling their demand of *paan* (betel-leaf) and *beedi*. As a result of these efforts, those cinema people would allow us to sit near that machine and then there was no limit to our divine joy.

When and how the information department people used to come was a matter of mystery for us. We felt good when they used to come and felt very sad when they left; but this sorrow would have been mitigated by Ramlila and Bhavaiwala; but about them on some other occasion.

My father had a government job, so when he was transferred from Dahod, we came to Halol. Halol is a village near Pavagadh, a sub-division of the Panchmahal district. When I came to this village, the taste of life in Dahod was intense. The sound of the anklet-bells of those Dheraiya Bhil brothers, the rainy tune of 'Jodiya Paava' of the young Bhils, the sharpness of their bows- and arrows and the sweetness of the corn-cob, the passionate and exciting songs of the Bhil girls—all that was together, and with us was our Lalji-Thakurji. Our parents firmly believed that it was Thakurji who used to take us from one village to another and I don't know why I never had interest in opposing this belief. Sometimes I prefer to be swept along by emotion rather than going against dry logic, even at risk.

□

3

Recently, last month, I was going to Baroda from Dahod in a bus, when I came across Halol in between. It seemed as if the face of this village had changed. When a teenage girl, who used to wear *choli-ghagra* (bodice and long loose skirt) and tie a bun, gets 'improved' after going to the city and comes out in a mini or maxi-skirt with 'bobbed hair'—I felt the same the feeling one feels at that time. The bus was moving on the road at high speed and I too was sliding past at the same speed with the help of something slippery. Along with the window of the bus, I opened the window of memory as much as possible, took out my eyes and tried to collect the past events and faces and began to attempt to making them present in front of my mind's eye; but the relentless speed of the bus was not conducive to this churning. How could I just call out to the driver and ask him to park the bus here or there as per my wish? I was silent and yet strangely outspoken enough to express myself while turning the ledger on the past. When the bus stopped at the Halol bus stand, I saw that many valuable things from the treasure of my past had been missing.

There was a humped tree near the present bus-stand of Halol. A small tree but strong! One of its branches was bent like the hump of a camel. When I entered secondary school, as soon as the recess was over, I would come running to ride on that branch of the tree. Generally, the rule was made that whoever came early should sit on it; but sometimes the rule of the jungle—two parts for the stronger—would also apply. If some elder boy would order me to stay down, then I would pray to God in my mind that this branch might crack and break. It's good that God does not listen to prayers made out of jealousy. If the branch had broken after listening to the prayer, I would have had to pray again for another branch to grow. Yes, it is such a good thing that I did not even go to pray that bad things happen to those elder boys.

Eating the breakfast brought from home on this humped tree, jumping up and down on this tree making noises like a monkey, and competing as to how much ground she can touch by bending that branch like a Shiva-*dhanush* (bow of Lord Shiva), was my favourite daily routine. We have held many serious conferences on this humped tree, and while doing so, have sometimes suffered the punishment for losing a period or two of school.

I remember, there was a boy in my class—Shanti! He used to come out of his home laughingly carrying a bundle of books and copies and a box of snacks in his bag. In class, prayer was followed by attendance in first period. After that, he immediately used to start feeling pain in his stomach. 'Golden' letters from his guardian were always ready in his pocket. He would give a letter to sahib with a kind face and then as soon as he got leave, he would carry his bag on his shoulder to go to the doctor. While leaving like this, if the person giving leave was not attentive, he would have created mischief. I knew very well that this fellow would reach that humped tree. He would spend a lot of time there. He would count the trucks passing by, take breakfast as early as possible and sometimes take some rest.

Today, that humped tree has fallen into the jowl of

time. Today I am a stranger to this land, but I know how much mischief I have created in the lap of this earth.

□

We once lived near the road leading from Halol to Pavagadh. During the peanut season, we would see trucks full of sacks being carried here and there. Our eyes were more on the sacks filled in those trucks than on the trucks themselves. There were big warehouses of sacks of peanuts near us. Sacks of peanuts would be kept outside for weighing during the season and our hungry group would start circling around like rats and squirrels. Initially, the effort was made to collect the peanuts that were spilled while weighing and filling, with the grace of the warehouse staff. There would have been humility in these doings, but where would there have been pride? That's why we had to immediately find holes and if we couldn't, make holes and then take up the adventurous task of taking out the peanuts. Our pleasure (or displeasure?) would be focused on that. For this we had to make full use of our investigative instinct, courage and tact. I did not think that this type of theft could in any way be considered a crime under the 'Penal Code'. For *jaggery* that perfectly complements these peanuts, we used to have to follow the same tried and tested way. When mother had gone out of the kitchen, at that time it became necessary to quickly put a big piece of *jaggery* in the pocket and leave the house quietly. A circle of friends used to be gathered outside to welcome and greet my successful endeavour. Our group would reach the banks of the nearby pond with peanuts and *jaggery* taken out from the sacks and gather there for half an hour or even an hour.

But the cruel and jealous Almighty does not tolerate such delightful adventures for long. I remember that once

I was caught red-handed by a warehouseman while taking out peanuts from a sack. He emptied all my pockets. Then not only the peanuts were lost, but the house's glorious *jaggery* also had to be lost. That rude warehouseman had given me a stern warning and said, "Being a devotee's son, aren't you ashamed of doing this? This time I am letting you go, if I catch hold of you again then it will not do you any good." Since that day, while buying peanuts and eating them, the pain of that incident gets mixed with it. However, today I am in the mood to taste that soreness too.

□

The chariots of Mataji (Mother goddess) used to pass through this road of ours many times and especially during Navratri. As soon as I heard the sound of drums and cymbals playing from somewhere in the distance, I would run and stand in the window. Mataji usually came down on those pulling the chariot, so they would walk beating their heads, a fringe of peacock feathers used to be in their hands. Some of the people too walking around used to beat their heads; they would jump while beating the head and also make loud noises; sometimes, the hasps would rotate and also hit. Mata's chariot, earthen-lamp, fragrance of incense sticks, atmosphere filled with *abeer* and *gulal,* special kind of rhythmic sound of kettledrum—a unique audio-visual form used to captivate us viewers. I used to be filled with mixed emotions of surprise, fear, excitement etc. Sometimes the women of the Sangha (organisation) carrying the Mata's chariot would also beat their heads. Some would walk with sprouts on their heads, some would shine a trident, and some would swing a lemon by placing it on the point of a sharp sword. I did not feel like taking my eyes off this Rathyatra (chariot-procession) but was also afraid to go near it. By the way, after seeing many such

Sanghas of Mata's chariot, I too felt like marching out a Sangha.

There was a boy named Ghanshyam in our group. He was an expert in beating head. Once the hair of the head was untied and left open, while hanging its hasp on the half-naked body, he started beating head and making loud noises. He signalled me to catch up. As I caught him up, he became more in beating his head. While singing, he kept putting peanuts and *jaggery* in his mouth and spread five-ten grains for people like us. At such times, the special sound that is made from the mouth—since I did not know how to do that, I used to play the canister with our *datoons* (wooden tooth-sticks) and step in rhythm with the Mata who came down on him. Once Ghanshyam's art of coming down of Mata on him was well established, we all were engrossed in it, meanwhile his father came from behind. Ghanshyam did not even know. One of us saw him. He immediately said, "Ghanshyam, younger Kaka!" And on hearing the name of the father, the Mata who had come down on Ghanshyam and he too, got shocked as if electrocuted and went away leaving the chariot made by us helpless. Quick-witted I too learnt that my happiness and wellbeing do not lie in facing the younger uncle, but in following Ghanshyam faithfully. I came to know that that day Ghanshyam was very late in reaching home. His mother, after swearing several times, assured that someone would not say anything, then after a lot of thought he carefully entered the house in the evening after the lamp were lit up.

□

While we were living in Halol, what was considered to be the most cultured part of life, yet a perverse and unpleasant event—going to school—happened to this innocent creature. Five-six years old, very thin body. Panty up to the knees, that too loose from the waist, which had to be put on again and again. Short shirt, two out of three buttons missing. And I am not even talking about shoes. Sometimes, the underwear and shirt would have patches. But there was no awareness in those days about clothes. If the buttons of the underwear were opened and a friend insisted that the 'post office' was open, we used to close the buttons. But in that too, there was no question of any kind of shyness, hesitation or alertness. Having or not having clothes was the same. While playing *hututu-kabaddi,* we used to take off our vest or shirt, but sometimes I also remember taking off even underwear and making fun while playing like this. There was no question of such alertness at that time, hence there was a lot of happiness. Although in the pond, there was no hesitation in taking off clothes from the body in enthusiasm to take bath even in knee-deep water on the *ghat.* After taking a comfortable bath and drying the body, there used to be the intent to wear clothes and go home, somewhat dirty. For us, that pond-bath was more glorious than the pilgrimage places of the seven rivers like 'Ganges, Yamuna and Kaveri'. Although I should say that my love for the pond of Halol did not become very strong. There were no lotuses in our pond; they did not have the vitality to survive the heat of summer. The pond of Halol did not seem to me to have the same glory and status as the pond of Kanjari, my next village. This pond was fine for women washing clothes and washing utensils, but it was a bit shallow for diving boys like us who are lovers of deep water—later I had been feeling so when thinking.

The same pond which took in its lap a five year-old boy, later also took in its lap a twelve year-old teenager going to high school. That pond has appeared different to me depending on the age difference. If I turned from a child to a teenager, would nothing have happened to that pond by then? Perhaps my enthusiasm, perseverance and efforts would be lacking in capturing what might have happened there. I don't know why that pond looked like a sterile woman to me. Her face seemed to me to reflect some unattained beauty of fruitlessness, which was more desolate in summer. I lived and played on the banks of that pond, yet I could not become of its.

□

4

The day I was sent to the children-school* may have been an auspicious day for my parents, but I find it to be the most inauspicious and dreadful day. Just as a cord is placed on the hoof of a bull or a horse, it was as if that day a cord was placed on the soles of my feet too. I did not notice much difference between the blacksmith who hammered the nails and the Punditji of my children-school. The way dogs run here and there after seeing the personnel of the dog-catcher's car, I too tried to do the same on the day when they started taking me to the children-school. I did not know Gandhiji, yet at that innocent age, with the same steadfastness as Prahlad, I had done a fierce Satyagraha for not going to the children-school. First, I remained disciplined and kept my feet steady, then I sat cross-legged and finally, by clinging to the hard ground with all my might, I made an unprecedented and final effort, but everything failed. According to Punditji's meticulous scientific information, I was carried through the market to his teaching-premises, swinging my arms and legs. Meanwhile, my lamentation about separation from home continued in a loud voice. My lament which even the stones of Bhavabhuti's time would melt did not have any

* The author here used the term 'Bal Mandir' in the original text. In Gujarati-speaking regions, the children-schools are generally called 'Bal Mandir'.

—Translator

particular impact on the audience; in fact, some of them were enjoying looking at my condition.

I had to go to the children-school against my will and sit there. Meanwhile, my mind, tired of mourning, got immersed in the serious thoughts of getting out of the boundary-walls of the school. My state of mind would probably be no different from that of Sita in the Ashokavan. Sitting in the school, I was watching with interest the monkeys jumping on the banyan tree in the distance and was drinking gulps of inspiration from them to run away from here.

The Punditji of my school looked as dull and hard as a dry cold chapatti. His elder son, Mana, was considered to be an enhanced version of himself. As records are put on the gramophone to play, in the same way, after making us sit to speak the table of units-tens, Punditji used to get engrossed in the work of book-binding with his son. Many boys would sometimes look out of the windows and doors with a stealthy glance and keep talking. Every now and then, if someone felt a gust of wind, they would suddenly wake up and sit straight, cross-legged, because of a sound like bronze while rubbing Punditji. I don't know why I found the entire atmosphere of this school uncomfortable and unemotional. The small dirty *pancha* gossiping about Punditji's miserliness, the sacred-thread exposing to be a glutton, the odd bi-coloured hair coming out of the nose and ears and the moustache like a spider's web on the ungainly face—I don't know why all this used to create a feeling of shapelessness in me. Seeing Punditji, the mind would shrink like a Japanese fan, the eyelids would become heavy with the weight of sleep. Yawning would come again and again and the body would not be able to sit straight cross-legged, I used to be desperate to get free from the clutches of the school's walls and at that time I would remember the efforts of my elder friends who were trying to take out the kite stuck in a tree. Actually, there was not much difference between my condition and that of that kite. The only difference was that the kite seemed capable of being removed from it, but I did not.

That school for children used to run from eleven to four o'clock, but every moment from eleven to four seemed as heavy as lead. The cows, buffaloes, sheep, goats and donkeys passing through the school also seemed very happy to me. They had no need to bother about studying throughout their life. Who invented this slate and chalk-stick? Man does not have the privilege of flying by spreading his wings even when he wishes to, like a bird. This is actually a grave injustice on the part of God on us, a grave oppression on us. A pinch of wisdom we got and we were overjoyed. But look at least, is there any place for our happiness?

After eleven o'clock, as the sun rose above the head, my boredom also increased, and there came a time when I would slowly slip away and reach the door on the way. And as soon as Punditji's eyelids became heavy after the meal, I too would cross the threshold and walk on the crooked path with the bag hanging on my shoulder. Roaming here and there, I used to look closely at the things in a shop, and if I saw a conjurer performing bear-or-monkey or similar magic tricks, I too would have joined his beloved gratis audience.

Once, while I was watching the conjurer's game, he pointed at me with his black shining eyes and said, "Look, I am placing a bird on the forehead of this child. Everyone should clap." And everyone clapped, I was very nervous and the conjurer laughed out loud and said, "Don't be nervous child, the bird is here in our pocket." And he showed taking out the bird. And as soon as he showed the bird—I too ran away, like a bird, from there in a hurry. After that, even in such shows, I used to prefer the position of a very careful observer.

But my experiment of the great renunciation of skipping school did not last long. Within a few days, Punditji had come to know of my 'hoaxing move'. The family members were also beginning to have doubts. There was no watch on my wrist and sometimes if I reached home before time, my brothers and sisters used to doubt, but I would talk about taking leave from Punditji on the pretext of being unwell. But this thing did not fit properly. My such 'experiments with untruth' did not last long. One day, when I crossed the wall of the school and took the path of 'enchanted wandering in the aimless world', I saw that I was not alone. Surrounding my path were the boys of the school, some more 'elder' and loyal than me, standing ready to catch me the way a fielder is ready to catch a ball or a crazy ball. I panicked; was caught in a fix. There was only one weapon left and that was to cry loudly, I tried it determinedly by lying in the dust; but I failed miserably. I thrashed my arms and legs several times like an octopus, but the grip of the five-seven boys was so strong that I became helpless. It was not possible for me to maintain the style of Poras who had lost to Alexander in the battle. Just as a running rat is cruelly caught and put back into a mousetrap, in the same way I was put back inside the school. I was looking with watery eyes at that innocent faces with a mixture of pity, compassion, ridicule, anger etc., which were shining around me. Punditji's fiery eyes were scaring me. I focused my eyes downward, lowered my head and started scratching the plaster with his toe. Just then Punditji's rebuke was heard, "Hold your toe-thumb." Immediately electricity ran down my spine. Becoming helpless, my existence bowed down.

Some time passed. I started having back pain. As I was about to stand up, Punditji's lovely and hurting stick hit my back and immediately I had to bend from the waist again in response to that. But now there was no such situation in which the toe could be held for long. I felt that being beaten with a stick was better than the torture of holding my toe. So I rebelled and chose to stand straight with tied hands. Punditji saw this. Perhaps he started feeling disobeying his orders. He came closer to show the stick. One...two...three—no resistance was there from me. I don't know how even crying had been forgotten. I remained standing as I was. Punditji shouted again, "Stay standing, beware if you sit." I don't know how such wisdom and courage arose in me that as soon as he said this, I quickly sat down. I saw that some of my child friends felt something like surprise and joy at this. Punditji was also stunned by this strange behaviour of mine, but immediately he swung a sceptre-like stick at my back. I was adamant, and he...? The broad-headed Punditji shouted for the third time, "Take him home." And immediately his group of grace-holding followers came into service. They almost dragged me out of the school. Later too, their wish was to drag me to my home, but I did not give them this opportunity. I myself ran towards home with my eyes closed.

As soon as I reached the door of the house, I thought, Punditji must have told father about my misbehaviour. I knew my father's anger. Nothing could be said as to when the Nrisimh-avatar would emerge in him. I acted with foresight and took my seat on the platform outside the house. With a dispassionate mind, I was sitting close to the pillar. I was just sitting and doing target-hitting with some pebbles. Just then, I saw father coming from distance. I immediately preferred to stand up quickly with my bag and stand at a safe distance from him. He looked at me and asked, "What happened in the school? Tell me" But I understood the situation, so I did not go near him. Father got angry and went inside. I felt relieved. I again took the pebbles and started doing target-hitting. The evening was spreading. The slow oozing of darkness had started. Stars were coming out in the sky after breaking the oysters one after the other. I was feeling hungry as well. The aroma of chapatti being cooked on the clay pan in the kitchen and the sweet sound of tapping it was making mye determined to go home wavering; but after seeing father's Rudravatar (manifestation of fiery anger), it felt safe to sit on the stairs near the platform of the house. I was busy watching the ploughs, bullock carts, water-carrying women and Bhils passing by the way. During this time, in my moments of carelessness, someone caught me from behind. He was my elder brother. A staunch supporter of father. I understood the situation. I started crying loudly, but it made no difference. Within moments I was thrown into the audience-circle of father. Just then mother, who looked as sweet as the smell of fresh chapatti, came out with flour in her hand. She said to father, "Don't beat him. He has been afraid for a long time." Father argued against me, repeated the stories of my valour, expressed concern about my future by saying that I don't study; and then mother shook her head, reminded of the God sitting on the throne with a thousand hands, evinced the thoughts of Vaishnavism and that softened my father a bit. Meanwhile, my younger sister came to change my shirt and showed my mother the mark of the stick on my back. Mother wept and said to my father, "Anyhow you meet the teacher and tell him not to beat my boy at all. Whatever complaint he has, let him tell us." Father also became softer after looking my back. The next day Punditji was summoned through the peon. Father gave him related information.

After this, I definitely received gentle protection from Punditji, but did not receive any affection. This hunger of mine kept on increasing since childhood—and I noticed that as much love I got, more than that I would beget insatiability. Does insatiability increase or decrease with affection? Will that love in which there is more insatiability be called true? Perhaps true affection is rare, this would be only an ideal. I don't know why, but my mind gets blocked when thinking of affection. Affection is not a matter of thinking but of experiencing, that's why this would happen. The habit of asking questions started in childhood itself, it has not been completed even today. Similarly the lacking of affection also started from typical childhood, where has that also been completed today? I believe that it may never be completed. But I do not want to tell the story of *Snehopanishad* (the enlightened scripture regarding love), I want to tell the story of *Vidyopanishad* (the enlightened scripture regarding knowledge); but it has become clear to me through experience that knowledge also doesn't stick, doesn't come off without love. I consider love to be a great source of knowledge for life. This knowledge-holder was invisible for me in our children-school itself.

I did not spend much time in that school. I had just learned alphabet-and-counting when the time came to leave that school for children.

□

5

Seen so many villages and cities, but Kanjari is still Kanjari. This village is two miles away from Halol, with a population of two to three thousand. It had got a status of *gram-panchayat (*village-council*)*, it had a *sarpanch (*head of village-council*)*—this was an important thing for me; but the most important thing was that there was a durbar-fort *(darbargarh)* in Kanjari. How is the fort? The fortress itself! But even today its glory for me is greater than that of Chittor fort. Its doors, its turret, its parapet—all these had filled the mind so much. How much the mind was attracted. The Thakur sahib of that durbar-fort was such a glorious personality for me. (Recently it came to light that he passed away.) He would come to the cricket field and we observers would watch his batting sitting in the ghost bungalow. He would hit the ball with the bat and my heart would soar. I don't know how much I used to pray to God in my mind so that the ball hit by him should not be caught by any fielder. I have been very thrilled to see the Red Fort of Delhi, but despite that, my small durbar-fort of Kanjari still shimmers in my mind as it is. Its thrill is unique.

There was a unique competition between this Kanjari and Halol. Halol's elephants and Kanjari's arrows—we used to say so. Our argument was that Kanjari's arrows would pass through the elephant. Many of our brave men would have excelled in studies, writing and sports; if there was any deficiency in this, it would have been compensated by our dignified durbar-fort. For me, Kanjari was as glorious as Pavagadh standing firm, five to six miles away from our village. Just as I used to stand in the window of my home and look at the fire of Pavagadh in the distance, in the same way, likewise I look at my village like a flickering lamp while standing in the dark foothills of the past. Today, like Birbal, I am deeply immersed in some cold and heatless pond; still, looking at that Kanjri with the eyes of imagination from a distant lamp, I am feeling something like warming. It seems as if I get the strength of steadiness to stay in this reservoir.

When my father retired from the government job and accepted the job at Kanjari-Darbar (the royal durbar of Kanjari), I have a vague memory of how we all left early in the morning in the durbar-cart and reached Kanjari. The road was as rough and dusty as a desert, enough for making aged-wood creaked. Green and dry fences on both sides. The thorny sweet bushes spread over the fence of Manila-tamarind *(jungle-jalebi),* acacia, reeds etc., and the spirited movement of the courtly robust bull. The anklet-bells would ring and keep whispering some sweet action in the mind. While sitting in the cart, I didn't even know when the cloud of sleep drenched me with its sweet shower. When my eyes opened, the drain of outskirts *(siwan)* of Kanjari, which we called 'Lendo', came on. The bulls moved back a little, the wheels slipped a little, then climbed the slope in front. Women coming to the pond after washing clothes or carrying water used to stand with their veils removed and look at us. "Aye, these are Tikamkaka's family-members, coming from Halol." Saying this, she would walk behind the cart while elbowing the other person and talking. By the time our unauthorised procession from outskirts reached home, half of the village must have come to know about our auspicious arrival. There was huge potential and efficiency in wireless communication in my village.

As soon as my Kaka (father) came to the village, he got down from the bullock-cart and was walking on foot along with it. Strong wheatish body. The muscles of his legs were very strong, his face was round, he had a red tongs-like *tilak* on his cranium and an old black cap on his head, his voice was heavy, he kept saying *Jai Sri-Krishna* and kept walking with enthusiasm. Along with working as a courtier in village Kanjari, he also accepted the responsibility of worshiping Thakurji in the Vaishnav-temple of the village with utmost devotion. Be it winter or sunshine, rain or storm, he certainly used to go to the temple, and without fail. In the temple, he used to sing certain *kirtans* as per the availability of time. It was his firm belief that he himself sang *kirtans* as per the ragas like Bilawal, Sarang, Bhairav, Khamaj etc. which were prevalent in Haveli-Sangeet*. Such interest and training in *kirtan* was developed in Halol. After retiring from government job, he started taking training in the Haveli Kirtan. Between Halol and Kanjari there is a place called Parbadi. There my father and one of his friends (a Gujarati teacher and the father of playwright Mr. Ramesh Shah) used to meet, sing *kirtans* to each other and practice the ragas of Haveli. Whenever father used to be in a good mood, he would teach us a few lessons about singing; in this way he would sing the tunes of his favourite hymns *(bhajans)* along with the words. He had memorised many hymns by heart. Sometimes, after narrating to him, he would ask us to sing in the same way. The tune *'Radheshyam Kaho...'* (say Radheshyam...) was very dear to him. Very often he would sing to everyone in the home.

---

* Haveli-Sangeet is a form of Hindustani classical music that originated from being sung in havelis (mansions). In this form of music, classical-music based devotional songs have been sung for Lord Krishna by the Pushtimarg sect of Vaishnavism.

—Translator

All of us were there at home, but the most important personality among us was Thakurji. Father used to take full care of what makeup He should wear on a daily basis and according to the season. Thakurji was also given the heat of a hearth in winters and at that time, we children used to have the audacity to steal the virtue of heat by sitting next to it for ensuring to keep the hearth burning. Father had written down detailed information about when and which dishes should be offered to Thakurji. According to this, he used to give instructions to the family-members regarding service. He used also to keep giving useful guidance to the priest of the temple regarding Thakurji's attire or material, etc.

It is not an exaggeration if I say that when my father came to Kanjari, the Vaishnav-temple over there really brightened up. He worked hard to ensure that various types of festivals were held in the temple. Sometimes, due to the good wishes of the durbar, he used to come running to the mansion even during office hours to serve that Thakurji, who is the durbar of the durbars. When it was lotus season, lotuses were plucked in large quantity from the huge pond of the village. With which Thakurji can be decorated. When the Rathyatra would come, we used to spend hours upon hours decorating Thakurji's chariot in the temple and swinging the carousel. If there was morning school, then the afternoon time would be spent in such fine service of the temple. Many times, the quadrangle of temple would be filled with hundreds of pitchers of water and Thakurji would be floated on a copper plate. When father used to sing the hymns of Thakurji's aquatic-dalliance with old round glasses on his nose, and if the plate would move a little due to some mistake of the priest, then he would see it through the upper part of the glasses that had fallen on his nose and while singing, he would shout loudly in between,

"Are you peeping here and there? If Thakurji had fallen now, it would have been a big disaster." Pujariji was used to father's harsh words, so without feeling bad in his mind, he would be careful and start bathing Thakurji more carefully. We Vaishnavs also take pleasure in floating Him who is the saviour of the entire world. This very is the oblation of our Pushti sect.

Father introduced a lot of new things into the temple. He used to give a good amount of his time to the temple for making beautiful *rangoli* (coloured-motif) for the Lord's *leela* in the evening. He used to take keen interest in the *darshan* (visitation) of carousel, cradle, bungalow, boat, etc. should be organised systematically in the temple. Once or twice a year, he also started an exciting programme of taking Thakurji's procession to some *bari* (enclosed space) through the temple people. Actually, he was only devotee coming and going to the temple; the administrators of the property, etc., of the temple were others, but when the time came and when needed, he would also interrupt the administrators and hence, if there was anything related to the temple, they would definitely take father's suggestions.

The main centre of father's flavourful life was the mansion. Sometimes, alone, especially on the day of cradle after Janmashtami, he used to invite everyone and dance—*"Nand gher anand bhayo, jay Kanhaiyalal ki"* (There became joy in Nand's home, victory to Kanhaiyalal). At that time, my fellow friends would also jokingly say, "Look, uncle has got some colour on him." I would have felt very ashamed then, but I was soft by nature, so I used not to like to argue over such a thing.

Father had a good influence on the Vaishnavs of the village. Even in that, the women had pure devotion towards him. At night, *satsang mandali* (the religious congregation) would sit at my place. Father used to read *Chaurasi*

Vaishnavon ki varta (talks of the eighty-four Vaishnavs) or something else, and if the Vaishnavs from the neighboring areas came, he would listen to them; from time to time, father would also do commentary on his own behalf. During this time, the rosary of *gomukh* also kept rotating in the hands of many people. The whole atmosphere seemed devotional. The kerosene lantern burning and in the dim light a boat filled with fifteen-twenty people floating in the waves of devotion—this is an unforgettable picture at least for me.

Whatever had to be done for Thakurji, father had a strong desire to do it with his body, mind and money. Mother's unsolicited support was also there. The effect of thrift was visible in our daily food, but not in the *prasad* offered to Thakurji. Despite our house being an ordinary one, out of all the donations collected for Thakurji and for Vaishnavism, its contribution used to be almost the highest. If any *Parivrajak Vaishnav* (wandering ascetic Vaishnav) came to the village, he was welcomed and respected in our home as per appropriate capacity. If any *Acharya of Vaishnav Sampraday* (learned preceptor of the Vaishnav sect) came to the village, he would be honoured with pomp-and-show in our home. At that time our enthusiasm also got reflected in the decoration of the house. A festoon would be placed on the door. Pavilions used to be made out of the *sarees* brought from home. The priest too might have been irritated to see that decoration. The enthusiasm with which my mother, my sister etc. used to sing might have increased his anger further, it seemed very possible to me at that time. Despite this, everything used to be completed well, the glow of father's *'Bhagatkaka'* pose kept increasing continuously. The belief of my mother, elder sister etc., had become firm that my father was some divine being. There is such an 'atheism' in me that till date I have not been able to gain the faith to look at any person with only devotion.

As soon as I came to Kanjari, the first thing I did was to visit my school. There was a good compound in front of the school building. I liked it very much, but there was a tamarind tree in its backyard and there was a strong belief that a ghost lived on that tamarind tree. We young children did not go to school alone. Sometimes even if someone went to urinate, we used to take the devilish pleasure of breaking his trance by calling him 'ghost'...'ghost'. The headmaster of this school lived very close to where we lived and this was the most regressive and objectionable topic for me. That teacher had the habit of finding out information about us whenever he came. Initially this habit was not particularly objectionable, but later it became unbearable. Whenever I got a call from the teacher's house, I would have to go, make rounds for his work, and if I complained about it, everyone at home would scold me, "One should do whatever guru says."

I remember that when I was teasing some teacher and drinking his juice of cracking-sound with concentration, I had to endure a strong slap from my father. I was beginning to develop the ability to use abusive language and that too was curbed by one such slap from my father. The strength of vim in my speech is less, if someone diagnoses its root cause by eliminating it, then without thinking more I would gladly declare my support to him.

As soon as I went to Kanjari, I once participated in the initiation-process of smoking. A teacher in our primary school was very addicted to *beedi*... every now and then, on the pretext of urinating, he used to go to the back side of the school and after taking a few puffs of *beedi,* he would come back refreshed. He was also quite harsh, so we disliked him a lot. We also used to undertake adventurous ventures to observe his *beedi*-lust. By picking up the stubs thrown by him in the backyard of the school, with the good-fortune of someone's yard fire, friends would sometimes indulge in the pleasure of smoking in the evenings. Once a landlord's son encouraged me to smoke. I pressed the stub between my lips as an offering to the teacher, but then I couldn't inhale it by holding my breath. Meanwhile, our teacher's carriage arrived there. His sharp glance fell on me and I threw away my stub and ran into the class; but as I pressed the stub between my lips, that dreadful scene came under the sharp gaze of our teacher. Because of this, he asked me in the middle of the class, "Being a devotee's son, you do this? I will have to tell your father." I was not in such a healthy state that I could say yes or no. I went home with a trembling heart and wavering steps. Keeping my bag at home, I took a book and banged it loudly on the porch of the house and then began reading. My only intention was to please my father. He used to read the best sources while walking in porch. He also told me a few times to read the text slowly. But I had to win his heart with my erudition. I continued my studies diligently and then amidst my shivering, the teacher, who was passing by our house, stopped, adjusted the white cap on his head and said to my father in a murderous voice, "Trikam-bhai, please interrupt him a bit. Today he was smoking a stub of *beedi*. I thought it was not right that a devotee's son should indulge in such an addiction." Then he had a brief talk with father. My situation was such that I felt I was sitting in the middle of a burning tunnel. Now it was very difficult for me to get up and run away. I kept speculating about where my father's slap would come from and on which part of my body it would fall . The teacher went and father picked me up by my arm and slapped me on my cheek. It seemed as if I was shaken to my roots, "Being a Vaishnav's son, you don't feel ashamed in roguery. Beware, if now you sit with those loafers." And from the second day in primary school, I had to sit in the front under the direct supervision of that teacher. Recess-ban was also in effect for me for some time. Then gradually I too kept becoming proficient in home remedies on how to maintain personal freedom even amidst father's Section 144. I started enjoying my father's strictness as well. And during this period my zest for life increased a lot, looking back today I feel the same.

□

6

School could never become the receiver of my love; despite this, it has been the foundation-stone of my childhood. Who knows how many colourful strings of small, big, sour and sweet memories wrap around it like a spider's web and shine. As soon as I remember school, the drowsiness of a long, lazy summer day fills my mind and body. That was our government school. The face-facade of a government school is different. Its white dirty walls, such cobwebs that would narrow the vision, such hard wood of its doors-and-windows that would make the mind heavy, and light-dark colours. Such a red slotted roof as if it was showing a red eye to the sky, the dilapidated coat-and-junkyard standing behind the school house tying the ghost-tamarind and its compound, such a blackboard that induces the eyes to sleep, yellow attendance-sheet, and the black-ink bottle and the red holder—all this is visible emanating from the face of the school. Here the student's attendance is important. Here the file is more trustworthy than the man. That building in the primary school indicates such a tantric devotion that even the mantra chokes! I successfully completed four years in it. Today I am feeling proud of that flickering success.

Whenever someone starts yawning upon hearing about school, his head and legs become heavy, his stomach starts aching, and even if there is hypocrisy in it, I have immense sympathy. If a child hurling hands-and-legs tries to not go to the children-school with the person taking him, then without thinking, I am in favour of the child. After my experiments of the great-renunciation in the children-school, I had lost faith in the elders of the home, so there was no expectation that they would accept my leave even in situation of illness or accident or something like that. At that time the school looked unpleasant even from a distance, but there was no other option. Had to follow what was written in destiny. On many occasions, I was taken to school like a parcel under the supervision of a peon. I was the son of a royal person, so I had some value. I was made to sit in school in such a way that I got the direct benefit of the teacher's attention. The teacher's beating was handed out only occasionally, and that too rarely. Because of this privilege of mine, I would have been the envy of many of my classmates through no fault of my own, but I was helpless. Many times, I feel that it would be better if the peon did not come with me, it would be better if I were not made to sit at a special place. But your wish does not find the desired result everywhere! Despite this, the peon's posting was lifted within a few days and I too heaved a sigh of relief.

Our school time was 11 o'clock in the afternoon, but some of us would reach there at 9:30-10 o'clock; not for reading, but for playing. We would go to the school coat and hold our meeting. If tamarind pods were collected, we would eat them. Along with that, I used also to finish my afternoon snack before the school started and then as soon as there was recess in the school in the afternoon, I would run home, pleading for extra breakfast by appeasements. Before the teacher came, the school room would be opened by his pilot student, who would come in jingling with a bunch of keys. Just like water sinks as soon as the door of a dam opens, the flow of us students would fill up to get a good place as soon as the door opens. There would have been scenes of all kinds of noise, fighting and bickering. A boy with lean body and mind like me used to have to endure more in this jostling. I might have got a better place than the one I had, but some powerful boy would have come and snatched my place just by the influence of his body and aggressive speech and as if he was giving me some grace-points, he would have given me a place somewhere behind him. Of course, when the time of the examinations arrived, such boys would have been useful in making special arrangements for students like us. Keeping in mind the convenience of being able to see and write the answers to exam questions, at that time we were respectfully given a good place to sit, but at such times, as per the justice of the maxim *'abhagiye ka dauna kana'* (curse of unfortunate person is one-eyed), the teacher would come and change our place as per his discretion and as if ink-stains would spread on the faces of those boys. Their anger towards the teacher used to be expressed through abuses mixed with the *garam masala* (hot spices) in singular-number.

I would have liked the service of the school bell and clock very much. I found the sound of the school bell to be very sweet. Sometimes, if the teacher ordered me to ring the bells, I felt like ringing two or five more bells than he told us to do. Normally, I got the chance to ring the bells only when those fat boys allowed me to do so. It is true that such an opportunity was available only by the order of the teacher.

As soon as I started going to school, I had already learnt the special task like watching a watch. On the pretext of taking a pee break, I would peek into the clock section and very quickly convey the news to the entire class in the form of ear-to-ear wireless as to how much time is left for recess or school. About half an hour before school let out,

I used to be ready to stumble out of school. Sometimes, if my impatience caught our teacher's attention, I would be punished for staying fifteen minutes more even after the school bell had rung. This used to be implemented by the teacher's pilot with that key-bunch. At that time, I used to become very upset in our hearts, but I was helpless.

I remember one teacher who was a little more unpleasant for us. Used to order a pot of tea from home in the afternoon. He would invite boys to his homes to get small work done and that too on the pretext of teaching. We used to get very irritated by this. He would teach for hardly half an hour and then his daughter-in-law would 'pass on' among us the wheat trays to glean. This work continued faithfully for a few days; but then we all saw that the teacher had developed this habit and hence one of the boys would deliberately let five to ten pebbles fall into the wheat while gleaning it. This teacher also had the habit of collecting new things from the students. He would say to someone, "Why, is the pigeon-pea ripe in the field this time or not?" He would say to the other, "Why Shankar, this time you did not get me tasted the ears of wheat." He would say to the third, "Why, did the cow at your home birth a calf or not? What if you give me one vessel of *ghee*?" In this way he had taken many people under his wing. Once, he asked a student to bring ivy-gourd. The next day the student did bring it. The teacher happily hung the bag he had brought on the handle of the chair. One of us, a boy from Baria, saw this bag. He had enmity with the teacher. Every second or third day he was a favourite object of the teacher's experiment of chastisement. Seeing the ivy-gourd bag, he thought of something and went out into the recess. From somewhere, he filled some bitter ivy-gourds in his pocket and when the students along with the teacher went out to clean the compound, he slipped these ivy-gourds into the bag out of their sight. No one knew this except two or three students like me. Next day the teacher arrived as usual. There was a stiffness full of redness on his face. We knew the reason for this and that is why we were smiling in our minds. The teacher got angry at the boy who brought two *sers* of ivy-gourds. He said, "Stupid! The ivy-gourds that I brought yesterday was somewhat bitter." He clearly denied this. The teacher became more irritated, "Scoundrel, you tell lie?" The teacher was blessed with both anger and Saraswati. He thought it best to remain silent. He made the student do the exercise of rising-and-squatting for a month or two. That year he had great difficulty in even passing the exam.

Our elder teacher (i.e. Acharya sir) was also the second incarnation of Durvasa. I used to shudder as soon as I heard his name. Seeing him passing by, we would turn aside. During the afternoon on a holiday, when the boys were making peg-top spin, if he passed by, they would quickly run away leaving all the peg-tops in the circle and the elder teacher would take all those away . The drawer of table in the school was filled with many such helpless peg-tops, but no one had the courage to take them. He was a strict teacher, but was expert in teaching subjects like mathematics. If any boy broke the discipline, he would be called near and the teacher would raise him higher by pinching his waist and thigh as if he was turning a key in the clock. Sometimes he would take a stick and punish some miscreant boy. To the elders of the home, he would also give appropriate advice and suggestions whenever needed regarding the boy. Sometimes, if our class-teacher did not come and we used to have to sit under the guidance of the elder teacher, our situation would be like a deflated balloon. It would be as though we were going to register our names in front of some big jailer! At that time, as the son of an employee of the royal durbar, I had a good reputation—especially as a scholar student. There was more energy in the mind than in the body. This would keep my finger always up to answer this teacher's questions. Once I was sitting under the guidance of this teacher when suddenly, he had to go out. Who knows how his eyes fell on me and he entrusted me with the responsibility of taking care of the class. I should have flatly refused; but could not open my mouth. As soon as he came down the stairs of the school, the class jumped like a spring bounces up when pressure is removed. My delicate voice did not reach anyone's ears amidst a huge drum-like sound. One or two boys took chalks and started drawing a caricature of the elder teacher. Two or three other boys opened map-rolls and started looking at them. Three or four boys started pounding bows and dumbbells. And one or two of them removed me and started opening the drawer of the teacher's table, finding good peg-tops, keeping them in their pockets along with even distributing as alms. Along with this, I was also threatened, "Beware, if you do backbiting to the elder teacher." My condition had become like a betel-nut caught in the middle of a nut-cracker. On one side, the elder teacher, on the other side, the miscreant boys. I, as if by narrowing my existence and making it as small as possible, kept watching all this hubbub as a witness. Gradually, the hubbub increased so much. Then one or two teachers from distant classes came running. They punished the entire class by making them hold their toes. They asked me the names of the miscreant boys, I did not tell them, so I too had to hold my toe. Seeing me holding my toe, my jealous classmates became happy. "This happened because of you", said some of the boys, and even started scolding me. Everyone's face became red because of holding their toes. Eventually everyone's patience came to an end. The entire class stopped holding their toes and sat down, except me. The visiting teachers became more irritated. Everyone along with me was punished by being made to sit cross-legged with hands tied. From experience, I felt that this punishment was no less than the punishment of holding the toe. That day, my heart became sour due to the disrespect of my fellow friends. I couldn't understand the reasons for getting scolded despite being innocent. But just like love, it must be difficult to find reasons for hatred too, isn't it?

After this, for some days it felt as if I should not go to school. But according to my family, school was the gateway to my bright future. They could not tolerate that I should come back through that door. Forcibly dragging myself, I used to go to school. Even if I was sitting in school, somehow or the other I would still go out. I used to enjoy watching the screaming monkeys who used to descend on the distant neem trees. Once I was enjoying this pleasure, I felt my ear being pulled by the teacher's hands. I didn't even know that the teacher had asked me anything. When I became inattentive, the teacher pinched my ear in such a way that the whole class burst out laughing and I became as pale as a extinguished lamp; but my fuming anxiety was not going to touch the teacher's eyes!

I used to go home after school, throw my bag in the hallway and while sitting at the door I for how long would the keep looking at the plough, wood, bullock-carts, lorries, people etc passing through there. Many times, I would chase the floating clouds returning in the sky. If it was the second date of lunar fortnight, father would make me see that while turning the rosary in the veranda in the evening. He also made my friendship with Venus and Mars. I vaguely remember that once in a while he had given me *darshan* of Rohini also. Sometimes I liked making friends with the clouds in the sky and the moon rather than with school friends. The bitterness of the entire school day was reduced a bit by sitting under the sky at the entrance of the house. Sometimes, when school was in the morning, I used to sit at the door in the afternoon heatstroke and would keep watching with curiosity the dust storms on the way, rising the ghosts; and if a carter from Mumbai, a bearer, a juggler or a magician had come in that as well, then aha-ha! When he returned to his camp after roaming around the entire village, I would follow his steps. I could have seen the juggler's or magician's show for free, but who would give me a penny or two to see the Mumbai car? This was a big question. Like flies buzzing outside for the sweets kept in the glass cupboard, I used to wander around the bioscope of that Mumbai carter. If someone watched it, I used to get details from him as to how it looked. Sometimes I used to become completely depressed; used to feel like crying. Once at home, I was beaten for being so stubborn, but I did not get any money and after beating me, even my mother started crying as if it was she who had been beaten; I remember this. For her, every paisa was like a precious brick to support the household. Once or twice the neighbours asked me to give money, then mother—and when I came to understand, I too—had for self-respect stopped myself from taking money; this has also happened. Despite this, I had definitely watched the Mumbai car in that bioscope—even if only a couple of times. Watching that car like this and listening to the flexible voice of the narrator—these two experiences are different. After years, I saw the real Mumbai car with my own earned money, but this car cannot be compared to the toy Mumbai car in that bioscope. Its journey itself was unique.

□

7

If there is any most important day in school life that I felt, it is the day of school inspection. As the day of inspection used to be approached, the school also started adopting new colours like a swan. Two to four potter boys used to be placed on the roof of the school and corrugated-terracotta-pieces got thatched by them. The school used to be cleared of cobwebs. The board used to be covered with solid black paint. When the letters were first written in it with white chalk, they would look like jasmine buds shining in the smile on the face of a beautiful woman of black complexion, or like moonlight flowers shining in the dark night. The work of pruning and trimming the gardens used also to be handed over to ten-twelve selected students; they would use all their artistic skills in making flower beds and planting trees, because this gave them an opportunity to escape from the boring thing like reading. Some boys with beautiful handwriting used to be given the task of writing good-thoughts on the cardboard. The born studious boys like us, we were assigned the task of narrating prose or reciting oral poetry out loud. Five to ten artists of painting and craft would get busy in beautifying the school. The wind of revolution as it were, used to be started blowing all around. Now more agility and intelligence used to be seen among the teachers too. Chairs, tables, stools, cupboards, windows, doors etc., used to be cleaned with wet clothes. The school bell used also to be cleaned of moss by scrubbing it with sour tamarind. The shine of the combined labour of our many hands was easily visible in it. The sticks, dumbbells, bow etc. gathering dust in the school bin would come out with a bang. At that time, we too would have liked to go to exercise rather than study. Whenever the teacher ordered us to go for exercise, we would all be enthralled and even in that, if he would ask us to bring something like dumbbells or bow, the enthusiasm would have increased. During the journey from the box to the school grounds, many of us used to play fine games with the rhythm of dumbbells or bow or with the stick game, and at that time the whistle of the teacher—who was standing at a distance and watching our rhythm—would sound like the sound of a squirrel and we would proceed going immediately and quickly stand in front of him in the queue like the black and white bands of a harmonium. After that, our rhythmic exercise used to be continued with the beat of whistles. Sometimes the sound of bugle and big drum would be added to it, and we would feel more excited and a kind of charge would be added to the exercise.

Like exercise, there used to be a lot of preparation for the cultural programmes like drama, dance, song, *garba,* etc. We had a girls' school nearby, where we used to practice *garba,* songs, dance, etc. We were young And till then, were not aware of the gender differences between men and women, and hence did not to feel any shyness, hesitation, fear or anger in going near or interacting with girls. The intoxication of that youth was unique. Whenever we got a chance amidst school work, we used to run also to enjoy the practice of those girls. The teacher would then interrupt, and we would turn back like a calf being pulled with a rope—keeping our eyes and ears in the same direction.

Thus, the date of inspection used to come closer and the

teachers would become restless. And the hustle and bustle used to increase. We studious boys used to be informed to prepare the questions-and-answers properly. Information used to be given to keep bags, clothes etc., organised. The first thing we used to do after going home was to search the bindings of books and notebooks. I used to get good bindings of books and notebooks from the royal durbar and the work of executing them was done by the peon; so it was easy. I used to carefully observe the way the peon did the binding and I too used to sit down to do the binding in the same way. The peon used also to enthusiastically try to keep me engaged in this work. After the books and notebooks were bound, the quick task was to write names, subjects etc., on them. What prestige would there be if the name, subject and other details were written in Gujarati? That should be written in twisted Roman script—in English only and then the help of father or elder brother used to be taken for this. After this was completed, I used to get some painting done with coloured colours or pencils from a painter classmate in exchange for five sheets of paper or two new coins or two peppermint tablets and if not so, it used to be done in exchange for a couple of *laddus* tied in Thakurji's sack. Books and notebooks would now be quite ready for inspection. Then used to come the turn of slate. The slate was first properly washed with coal water. If necessary, a piece of soap was also used. After that, ripe leaves of *thuhar* would be brought and its body would be massaged with them. After that, the castor would be rubbed to make it a little greasy and if the pen still refused to move on it or be visible clearly, it would be massaged again. An hour used easily to be spent in scrubbing and coating the slate with various liquids and bathing it. When the slate work was finished, it used to be time for the bag. Mother or sister would sew the school bag at home. Generally, torn trousers, tights or pyjamas, bedsheets etc., were used in it. The kind of beautiful bags that are available in cities today were not even dreamt of at that time, but small tin boxes or plain leather or jean bags were occasionally seen in Bohra's shops. I was very keen to get one or two tin boxes, but this remained only in my mind. I had a homemade bag. If I had insisted a lot, mother would have made a new bag, that was all, but I saw that my situation even in this matter was relatively very good.

I used to see around me such children from the community of Baraiya, potter, barber etc., whose bags would have so many holes that even the books would be visible outside and yet they would not be repaired or even washed properly. Whoever poverty catches, it catches with full love. Its form is reflected not only in a man's face but also more-or-less in the things he uses. There were students with me who did not even have oil to put on their hair, among them who became my friends, on the day of inspection someone used to come and say to my mother, "Aunty, deputy sahib is coming today, could you please put some oil on my hair.?" They would get the oil poured from my mother—and my mother, who could not tolerate even a drop of oil falling down, used to pour the oil with amazing generosity.

Thus, by the time the inspection arrived, we students used to be prepared like disciplined soldiers, after which we would start eagerly waiting for the Inspector sahib's ride.

In our village, Bapu's ride on Dussehra, Varghoda of Shivratri, *taziya* procession, similarly in other villages, Bapu's motor-vehicle used to come and in that too, the head of any tiger or nilgai that was killed after going hunting, used to be placed on the roof of the motor or on the bonnet along with the flower garland in such a way that the whole village could see it and when Bapu would come to the village, the puppeteer's weak but delicate mare used to go jingling and waving the red-and-yellow clothes—the way these were glorious events for us, in the same way, when under the shade of a black umbrella our elder teacher spreading a new carpet used to get down with the renowned deputy sahibs of our school at the door of the school who were made sat on the durbar's bullock-cart, this was a very glorious incident for us—should be said supernatural!—'Look-look, the Nal* has arrived'—like that. As soon as deputy sahib alighted at the door, bugles and big drums used to start sounding and with this the voice of the drill-teacher would burst. Along with this, the sticks of the queues facing each other used to rise high in the air which would cease after making a triangular arch and below it first the teacher of the school, then Bade sahib and then deputy sahib and along with him his madam *sahiba* would come. Whether the deputy sahib is from abroad or from here, for us his wife i.e. 'madam'. In our eyes, it seems as if they were people from some other planet. There used to have been some students among us who would have thought that one of the sticks raised high in the air would fall on the shining bald head of some deputy sahib. After deputy sahib left, some of us used to laugh by imitating him and madam exactly. Many of our teachers laughed seeing this free entertainment of ours. Still, they diligently used to keep a serious face, ignore us despite looking and then pass by.

The way our elder teacher and other teachers used to follow these deputy sirs, I felt bored towards the deputy sirs. How could our lion-like teacher move like a jackal? How could we tolerate this? But due to the feeling of respect towards him, we also used to sit and behave decently in

* 'Damayanti Swayamvar' in 'Nalakhyan': Damayanti being thrilled on the arrival of Nal.

front of the deputy. The deputy sahib would stay for a day or two, during which time we would feel that the condition of elder teacher was as if a girl was getting married at home and the girl's father wandered around restlessly carrying the whole house on his head. The deputy had to be served tea, water, snacks, food, etc., at the right time. Two or four loyal and experienced boys used to be kept in his service.

The welcome and farewell ceremony of the deputy sahib also used to be celebrated with great pomp. The village-head, *patwari,* police-Patel*, Babaji of Ramji-temple, *seths* of the village and elder Bapuji from the royal-durbar, younger Bapuji and their five or ten relatives along with the manager would be present. Starting from my father and others, a squad of three to four peons also used to come to this function. I used to have more fun seeing Bapu and his relatives with their heads hanging down to their waist and the crest taken out from the turban on their heads. The younger Bapu used to have a sword with a silver handle in his hand. Behind, one or two persons used to have guns in their hands, one or two would have a spear in their hands and the ride would reach the gate of the school. The elder teacher would bowing welcome Bapu and the air used to echo with thunderous sounds, then even the birds on the tamarind tree would start chirping. I would watch all this with great interest. For me at that time, even more important than deputy sahib and Bapu would have been the gun-shooting peon, whom we can call Zafar Khan for convenience. What surprised me at that time was that... Zafariya—who was going this morning through the royal-durbar smoking *beedi* and wearing a round black cap like bitten by a rat with the dirty *kurta*-pyjama and carrying an

---

* A non-governmental position prevalent in Gujarat, who on behalf of police looks after the village and mediates between village and police. —Translator

oil can on his shoulder—now being dressed up in military attire, carrying cartridges slung over his shoulder, tipping of his moustache, used to fire the gun with much pomp-and-show. For me, this gunman Zafar Khan, those spears, swords, the turrets of that durbar-fort and Bapu sahib himself were the centre of ultimate identity and mystery. My childhood mind was filled with humorous stories about all this. I used to like to stand in front of that Zafar Khan. Only then, if our teacher would not force me to sit at the designated place in the school ground.

As per tradition, the ceremony used to begin with the welcome-address by the elder teacher. Bapu sahib would be the president. Our elder teacher's Saraswati used to shower with full force on the deputy sahib and Bapu sahib. Then another teacher of ours used to take charge of the inauguration. Whenever cultural programmes of our students were presented, the names of the students used to be called and some would get up enthusiastically while some would get up trembling as if they were being brought to the slaughter-pillar. Somebody used to speak the dialogue in an overbearing voice. Somebody would pretend. Some would recite poetry and some would narrate prose. Somebody would tell a joke or a story and in this way, everybody would come back after doing their duty—as if somebody had removed the load of grain from the back. Then there used to be songs, *garba* and dance. Distinguished guests used to be honoured with flowers. Then the exercise experiments used to continue and there would be warmth in the environment. After that, the deputy and the chairman used to speak. In the meantime, many like me used to have got absorbed in such other tendencies not by body but by mind, without being caught by some one or the other sahib, and ultimately everything would have been completed with great pomp-and-show. And as a witness to this, the spongy-sugar-cakes or something like that used to be distributed from the royal-durbar's side. And our mind used to become blossomed with the spongy-sugar-cakes received in the form of this auspicious bright-benefit of our *bhagirath-tapashcharya* (the deep penance as performed by Bhagirath) and sunlight-practice.

And in the end... just as the sky becomes clear after two or three days of continuous rain, there is shining sunshine all around or as if the eclipse clinging to the neck of the Sun or the Moon is released, as soon as the departure of the 'deputy sahibs'—similarly all of us, even our teachers, used to feel relieved and feel a reassuring peace as if the school had emerged safely from the storm, its bad omen had abated or an ambush had been averted. After the inspectors left, the school used to go on for two-three days just to say, our teachers used to spend their school-time in enthusiastic discussion about the inspectors and their respective talents, and we used to have been able to imitate 'those deputy sahibs' and used to spend by mind-voice-action our time relishing the programmes that took place by presenting them in various forms. I can never accept school inspections just as I can't accept a lock. This tendency of inspection is a clear indication that something is lacking in the very foundation of our proclivity of learning, something is wrong and something has gone bad. The way schools should be run, but today there is a fear that along with the devotees and priests, even the gods might become corrupt. Now, again and again I feel that what we learnt cannot become unlearnt. Who will have this herb? Even today, I am in search for it.

□

8

Recently I had gone to Abu in the proximity of stone-made Goddess Lakshmi. Stones have their own different beauty. They have the unique ability to make people happy. Through the contact of stones, some hidden beauty of forest and water emerges. Due to the abundance of stones, being enriched with dignity and glory, they transform into the extraterrestrial *girilakshmi* (Lakshmi in the form of mountains). For me, this is the interview of Parvati—the daughter of the mountains' emperor. The tinkling of anklet-bells of that Parvati is within the range of hearing at every waterfall. The tinkling of anklet-bells itself inspires me in the rocky caves of childhood, in the hilly creation of Pavagadh where its original source is like a casket of remembrance of childhood. Many miles away from Abu, and even then, for me, as close as my heart. Ahmadabad would be far from Abu, certainly not Pavagadh. If that *todarak* jumps, it would fall into the milky pond of Pavagadh only.

Even though Pavagadh is six to seven miles away from my village Kanjari, I never felt this distance. We used to debate many ways while watching the fire in the forests of Pavagadh from a distance. On the day of Holi, in the evening, during the twilight, we would squint and try to see the Holi lit at Pavagadh through the greyness of the sky. At that time, we did not have telescopes or binoculars, but definitely had the art of vision inspired by the power of keen imagination, which gave us the power to see as per our wish. Thus, despite being physically far away from Pavagadh, the universe of my childhood was profoundly compiled with it. No conflict used to be there in my mind while handing over the flowing water from the outskirt of our village in the rainy season with a crest of dirty foam to Vishwamitri of Pavagadh. I used to have no problem at all in mingling up the steadfastness of Pavagadh into the steadfastness of our small durbar-fort. We had an enchanted belief that there are such tunnels in Pavagadh, one of which opens somewhere in the durbar-fort. We would not be satiated talking about Khapra Kodiya*. We recognised Khapra and Kodiya as bandits. By the sound of their mares' hooves our homeland used to be echoed. Due to the shine of their sharp swords, a festoon of severed heads of terrorists would be tied at the entrance of our village, which we would see. Due to the arrival of these rebels, our durbar-fort was sitting like a dandy who being dazed wakes up from opium sleep. The weapons kept in our durbar-fort used to have gained momentum. The tip of the spear used to start bouncing in the air. Daggers and swords used to generate electricity in the air. The barrels of the guns used to be showering bullets with fire and smoke from the slanted holes of our durbar-fort. The cannon used to start roaring from the turret of the fort. The palisade of dense-foliaged banyan tree of our village started trembling. A saffron young man with flowing locks would shoot like an arrow, sitting on a dashing horse. Sati Mata used to come out with *kumkum tilak,* long hair open on her head and an open dagger, garlands of torches would move in the air, red *gulal* and drums would spread a lot of excitement in the atmosphere and when our brave Khatariji used also to join it riding on *leela* horse, then with the sound of battle-horns and drums, a unique rhythm of

---

* Names of two bandits popular in the legend.

fight would arise in my veins. Many of my nights used to be filled with the sagas of Pavagadh's bravery and many dreams were transmitted to my mind, creating a grand and heroic universe from the ruins of Pavagadh.

Just as Pavagadh was apparent to me, similarly *Mata Kalika* (Mother Kalika) of Pava was also evident to me. In our village, *mandva* used to be crafted during Navratri. Before the days of Navratri started, I used to take out wooden *mandvi*. Used to take it to the pond and clean it thoroughly. I used to rub oil and diligently remove the dust from it. A quadrangle seat of wooden. Elephant in the middle and the pillar to place earthen-lamp on it. I used to decorate *mandvi* nicely with flowers. After fixing the bar-stand, the earthen-lamps used to be placed on it. It used to have been a wonderful event to ask for *ghee* and oil for those lamps. Prudence was used in asking for *ghee* and oil. An old mother—prosperous by family—used nonetheless to turn a deaf ear in giving *ghee* and oil. She used to give half a spoon *ghee* and that was not acceptable to me. When the old lady used to go out of the house to have *darshan* of God, I would reach her daughter-in-law and she used to pour in my can of *ghee* and oil more generously than necessary.

Whether I had eaten at home in the evening or not, I would have reached the pavilion. To make the *mandvi* of our locality look more magnificent than the *mandvi* of another locality, we used to do intense endeavour for this. We used to try to keep the place around *mandvi* clean and beautified, decorate it with flags and festoons. Then, to ensure that royal-durbar sahib came to our pavilion, our elders would make rounds and think about celebrating the festival of the pavilion in a grand manner. As the seventh-eighth date of Navratri approached, the *garba-garbi* around the pavilion used to gain momentum. People of all castes used to participate in it. There would have been courtiers and also

Baraiya-Dharana. Upper caste and backward people, men and women, young and adults all used to join in this *garba-garbi* without any discrimination. Rawal, the drummer of the village, used to add tune to it with two-headed hand-drum and siren. The *tabla-tansa* of the hymn-troupes used also to be played in it and the whole atmosphere being filled with *abeer-gulal* would sparkle like the Mother's nine-coloured *chunari*. Many of my friends used to get intoxicated with the fun of this *garba* and join in it. A *garbi* like *'dham-dham karti mede chadi, aina jhanjharno jhamkar, halwa jhulan jhulo'* (the jingle of her anklet sounding *dham-dham* climbs the attic, swing the hammock slowly) used to be sung. The brass pot used to be filled with Water. The *talaiya* would be filled with milk and *pari* used to be made with sugar-candy. *'Jay Mahakali, tera khappar na jay khali'* (victory to Mahakali, your cranium shouldn't be gone empty)—thus that Mahakali of Pava used to be invited to play *garba,* and the *garba* used to continue for three days and nights continuously on the seventh, eighth and ninth days. Everyone taking part in it used to get a well-cooked meal of *laddus* and rice mixed with lentils from the durbar-fort. The entire village used to roam and play around the pavilion like a potter's wheel or like a constellation. The carafe of colourful *chunari* and trumpet turban used to sway in the wind. In some events, Mother and Bhathi Maharaj used to come down to play *garba*. There used to be incense-sticks, earthen-lamps, offerings of worship and thus work, business, education and everything used to come to a standstill. There used to remain only the action of stomping of feet and clapping of hands, voice of throat and twisting of body parts. The entire village used to play *garba* and yet no incident of rudeness or molestation would take place there. At that time there was no electricity, no mike, yet there was not even an iota of lack in light or sound-splendour. Song in the throat, and love in the heart—for the great Mother Ambika *(Mahamaiya Ambika),* for Kalika.

Whenever someone from the crowd of this pavilion used to take up the *garbi* of Mahakali, then the picture of the entire incident of Pavagadh would play in my enthralled mind. We used to see the fearsome Kalika being taken down from Gabbar* in the form of a beautiful woman wearing a head-garland, and would see her coming near the playhouse of Patai Rawal. Due to her divine appearance and influence, Kalika was seen apart among all the beauteous women roaming around *garba*. Patai Rawal's lustful gaze does not go away from her and in that imaginary picture, the picture of the play of Kalika and Patai Rawal that the Bhavai-folks had performed in the village gets mingled up. The dandy-turbaned Patai Rawal grabs the scarf of Kalika. Kalika takes the form of fire from flame. Patai Rawal and with him his entire Pavagadh quakes to its roots. Large stone blocks roaring from the top fall into the elephant-deep gorge. The door is about to break. It seems as if the staircase turns upside down. The marble pillars of Patai Rawal's playhouse burst like banana trunks. Patai repents. He falls at the Mother's feet, but whatever was meant to happen, takes place. Pavagadh falls. The demonic power is defeated and the divine power ultimately wins. A legend of such sort emerges from every stone of Pavagadh and drenches our childish mind.

We used to relish the story of this Pavagadh-fall in many ways. Not only did we sing the *garba* of *'Maa Pava ne Gadathi utriya'* (Mother got down from Pavagadh) sometimes we even used to act out the entire story. Some of us used to dress up as Kalika, hang a tin tongue in our mouth, swing a sword made of cardboard, while others would hang the head of a pot with holes in our hands.

---

* The valley, where Mahakali resides.

Pavagadh used easily to be built with the piles of bricks-and-mud and heaps of sand. There were no less people competing to become Patai Rawal. Turban, dhoti, waistband etc. used easily to be obtained from the covering sheet. The lid that held the paint-box used to have made a shield and the strap for fitting the butt would have made a sword. Patai Rawal's army used thus to become ready. Mother used to come. Patai Rawal, like the hero of that play (Bhawai), used to be ready to grab the Mother's hand while circling the *garba,* then the Mother would start beating her head in anger. She used to play with a shield made of cardboard and unfortunately, if it broke due to being played in the wrong way, the Mother's anger would not be assuaged despite attempts. Five or seven of us used to hold the Mother by her arms and waist. This used to make Her jump even more. Patai Rawal used to roam around swinging his sword and then he would appear in the form of King Muhammad Begada wearing a triangular cap. Slogans—like 'Allah ho Akbar'! and 'Jai Somnath'!—used to be raised. The Mother while running used to disappear behind the tree. Patai Rawal used to express his readiness to accept defeat on the condition that he would act as Muhammad Begada in the next Bhawai-play. The tip of Muhammad Begada's sword used to hit his chest and our game would end there. In this game we could not dress Mother Kalika in a completely beautiful dress. We would have to admit this with regret.

We took the revolutionary idea of casting only women for the female characters in our such plays. Some girls were contacted, but mostly the party in front remained hesitant and uncooperative in this matter. It was a universally accepted policy that girls should not join the group of such spoiled boys. *'Chhokra bhegun chhokario ani mao bokadio'* (go with the boys, the girls are their mother goats)—this type of low grade sutras were prevalent. Due to this, we constantly used to feel the lack of female characters. If any brave girl used to be ready to play a female role, her friends would gossip about her audacity in front of the elders and as a result such a brave girl would have to live under the strict control of the elders. Our helplessness indeed deserved the sympathy of all those who cared, but how many such large-hearted people were there besides ourselves?

But we unexpectedly got help in another way regarding the female character. There were two or four born actors in our group. One was Soni's son. By stretching the covering bed-sheet over the head like a veil, he used to imitate like the female characters seen in the Bhawai-play...! His ability to make his eyes dance and present a feminine posture is still remembered. He used to show off the moves of different types of women; even the gait of a pregnant woman. We used to double over laughing after seeing this gait. The second one was the son of a Brahmin. His mother was not at home. Mother's clothes were kept carefully. Sometimes, he used to bring those by pinching them from home and play the role of a woman happily wearing those; however, in our personal meeting—in someone's closed room or in someone's enclosure. In front of appreciative spectators like us, he used to sing happy songs and dirges in women's voices. He used to pretend to beat his chest. Once he was engrossed in such acting. We too were completely lost in the magic of his acting skills when we heard a voice as if tearing apart the curtain of a drama; someone thundered, "Where has the whore died..."—and then what happened...! Our companion did not even have time to remove the woman's clothes; along with the voice of the most-revered father, his auspicious figure also started appearing. And he jumped over the fence and ran away. His capital—underwear-and-shirt—was with us. That's why we also ran away, giving up the benefit of the after-sight. That day, we had to put in special efforts, also by his father to find our woman-dressed Brahmin-consort. With great difficulty we could deliver his original dress to him. After this it was heard that he had to try to stay away from his father for two or three days at a stretch.

Our group used to take part in not only the plays of Patai Raval but also in some plays based on stories like Ram-Ravan, Bhim-Arjun, etc. In the play of kidnapping of Sita, our lean Ravan fell down while lifting the heavy Sita, I have a comically tragic memory of that incident. Such is the memory of the fight between Bhim and Arjun. I, packing *puris* from home, had taken *prasad*—for these theatrical-braves. There was fierce disagreement over its distribution. Bhim's argument was that he should get double the share of that *prasad,* because he himself is Bhim. But Arjun displayed fierce opposition to this and due to the instigation of the character Draupadi, this opposition reached the point of quarrel, as a result of which our group was divided into two parts for some time. In the end, one such leaf-bowl of *prasad* allured everyone to gather forgetting the past.

Once we boys adopted an auspicious resolution to enact the scene of Lanka-burning by Hanuman in the Ramlila. Among us, there was a well-built son of farmer, who always came first in high and long jump. We made him Hanuman And made him wear a nice cap and tied a loincloth. He hung the tail of the string around his waist, but tied it on top with a bamboo splinter. Someone's house was being plastered with yellow mud on the occasion of a marriage. We stole a box of yellow colour from there and applied it evenly on his body. Also applied some vermillion and *gulal* on his face; and thus prepared our Bajrangbali. One of our enthusiastic friends also made him wear a garland of crown-flowers around his neck. Now the important problem remaining was that of mace. What to do? We brought a stick used in playing *gilli,* inflated a big balloon on it and tied it and as soon as having prepared the mace placed it in Hanumanji's lotus-hands, Hanumanji jumped making a noise. He jumped up and reached the roof of the school's water closet. It was not difficult to jump from there to one roof, then the other. Hanumanji kept jumping on the roofs and our group kept standing below, roaring in his voice. The play was perfectly enacted. Our monkey-fellows were getting food-items like obtuse-leaved mimusops, manila-tamarind, roasted chia-seeds from the active appreciative observers. We used to throw food-items and he would catch it, showing his teeth and saying *'khon-khon'*. Whenever he jumped on a roof, the family-members of that house used to shout at the sound, so leaving that roof, he would reach another roof. Hanumanji was in great ecstasy and while brandishing his mace with pride he threw it on the slant wall of thin metal-sheet. The balloon burst and the mace was crushed. Hanumanji seemed to have lost half of his intoxication and his elder brother—who normally used to be in the farm at this time—suddenly arrived, as by luck this holy *darshan* was in his destiny. Our Hanumanji almost became in a fix. He stopped jumping and started running. Behind was the furious voice of his elder brother following him. At last, Bajrangbaliji hid in an old woman's manger. He washed his head with the water kept for the cow to drink; but there was no chance to change clothes. He spent some hours in confusion. The elder brother left angrily saying, "Come home you bastard, I will peel off your skin." We went to our Bajrangbali with full sympathy after finding out him. We helped him in every possible way to come back in his original guise; but the shivering of his mind and body was intense. Even after donning the original attire, he had to wait to enter the house for a long time by maintaining 'aesthetic distance' away from his residence. That day, returning to his house had become much more difficult to him than the entrance to Lanka. Finally, after the persuasion of one or two kind elders with polite words—like "It happens, they are boys, if at this age they won't do mischief, when will they?" etc.—their anger was calmed, then he was able to step into his home.

I do not know where that friend of ours is today, and that is why perhaps his brave friend, a werewolf, is still restless in my inner world. When will that friend of his meet him, and perhaps even if he does meet, will he be able to meet him in the way he used to meet him before?

□

9

I Just met a sister, she had come with some questions related to children's literature. Answering, I said to her, "Sister, if there is no love for children among those who wish to create children's literature, nothing can be achieved. Recognising the child within you and maintaining a close friendship with him—this is a very big thing. After growing up, there is a big difference between being like a child and being unintelligent. If being a child disappears when you grow up, then I will not accept such growing at all." These thoughts are from today, when years have passed since my childhood. When we were children, who had the time or inclination to think about whether childhood is a form of joy or a form of punishment?

At that time, food, sleep and fear—all three had a unique taste. Even of fear? Yes, the taste of fear too. At that time, the sweet sprinkle of sleep on the balcony due to the wave of moonlit-wet wind...! Some mysterious fragrance of dreams that floats in the air like a light sneeze...! Who knows when a sky-fairy having come used to make us lie down into a delightful swoon with her magical touch, we would never know about it. We used to enact new and novel plays in the streets of dreams. In the dream, there used to be a big crowd of plays and players. The princes running on white horses, the fairies with golden hair, the grandfather and the dervishes with their huge white beard entangling the entire sky—there were so many such characters crowding there. If we asked for grapes, bunches-after-bunches of the grapes used to burst out of the air. And their sweet juice used to fall drop by drop on the lips. If we sat in a flower, its wings used to start fluttering like butterflies. As soon as we sat on the swing, we used to reach the attic of the sky. In this play of dreams, it was not known when the morning came like the golden edge of screw-pine leaf.

In the morning, I would curl up on the bed and lie wrapped in a sheet, and the golden strips of sunlight used to spread out on the bed. I used to feel its warm touch on my face and a faint sense of awakening would start creeping into my eyes. The eyelids of the eyes want to remain closed like the safe of a miser, but after the mind has opened, it used to be difficult to keep the eyes closed. I definitely used to try to stay nine yards away following the ostrich's art in the morning by covering my face with whatever sheet, blanket or pillow came to hand, but I would not be successful. Some unseen hand used to pull not only the bed-sheet from under me but also the bed and make me roll from my sleeping-posture. The vessel of my sleep used to shatter into tiny pieces of glass and dissolve in the air. In front of me, the bright sunflower-like sun used to keep smiling softly. But I used to keep grimacing; used to make a valiant effort to hug the floor while yawning after yawn, but that too would prove to be short-lived. My sleeping-pleasure used to be vanished like a scarf of dew. I used to have become like *'Niralamba Saraswati'* (Saraswati hanging with no support). Nothing used to be understood, nothing used to be interesting . Then some harsh, supreme-authorised hand used to insert a wooden toothbrush of *kanasi,* neem or banyan-acacia into my mouth and the flavour of my morning used to be completely ruined.

During winter, I used to camp in front of the stove in

the kitchen of the house with something like half a bed on my shoulder. There used to be a pot of water on the stove and the crackling of firewood like castor and *senta* in the stove would be heard. Some *senta*-sticks were hollow in the middle and a light puff of smoke would come out of those. I used to keep such *senta*-sticks in my mouth like *beedis* and suck those in style. Why should I remain alone in such a tasteful matter? I used to keep the other four to five sticks burning ready for our sympathetic friends nearby. Once, our non-violent, egg-like innocent smoking party was perfectly going on and it stung the eyes of a cataract-hit old-woman living in our neighbourhood, that's it...game over...! She started shouting loudly: "Scoundrels! Don't you feel ashamed of being a *baniya's* son for sucking *senta* in your mouth? Should I put fire in your mouth? Get up and run away, otherwise I will call your mothers." We did not consider it appropriate to argue with the quarrelsome old-woman. As soon as the hot water was splashed, we were filled with smoke like untimely extinguished wood, yet we remained silent and kept waiting when the golden and unique opportunity do come to take revenge on that old woman; and such an opportunity came soon.

This was the occasion of Holi. Holi does not come only on the full-moon day of the lunar-month Phagun; as soon as Phagun started, we could see its golden-orange face; from then onwards we used to start preparing for Holi with great concentration. Collecting cow-dung from everywhere, my sisters would start making delicate and tiny *chipariyas*-and-*gujaris* with such holes that those could be stringed into twine. Like any security officer, I would take effective measures to ensure that these *gujaris* are properly dried. I used to be concerned about how long and big the garland of *gujaris* should be. Then we used to organise secret meetings to discuss seriously what items should be offered during

Holi. Many of us unpaid spies would provide exciting news as to whose house, enclosure or street has combustible material. After this, on the basis of our rich experiences throughout the year, we would make a list of those who harassed us, threatened us with false pretences, and were thus 'infamous' people who disliked us to the core and seemed doubtful of loyalty towards us. According to this list, it would be decided from whose place, when and in what manner, what things should be picked up for Holi and in how much quantity. After this, at the time of selection of selected workers from our group to complete this serious mission, I used to try to remain as far behind as possible and because of only that fear, I would experience great thrill of such work; but when it came to taking risks, I used to shy away. If there would be no such tendency of retreat in life... but now where are those days...?

We used to organise, a week in advance, a systematic strategy to steal firewood for Holi. This strategy would remain completely secret. For example, I remember that the son of the owner of that enclosure—from whose enclosure it was decided to be picked up for Holi—was also involved in our conspiracy and he himself gave invaluable guidance in the plan of picking up the plank. What cruelty he had for his domestic things, and what immense love he had for our congregation! In our meeting, we adopted a strong resolution to dig up the wooden door-frame that was used as a staircase in the old lady's house and burn it in Holi. The old lady was alone. She used to sleep on a cot made of twine in the backyard of the house. This door-frame was to bring after removing from the front part. A friend and I had to keep a careful eye on the sleeping old lady. It was the adventurous others who did the rest of the difficult work.

And finally, the colourful day of Holi arrived with much fanfare. The colour of *abeer-gulal* was set with the sound of drums. Ahead of Holi, a crowd of people was gathering from every locality and suddenly, breaking through the crowd, the old lady's door-frame raised on strong wooden stick was quickly brought into the spirit of martyrdom to be burnt on Holi. The boys kept laughing, saying *'Ram bolo, bhai, Ram'* (say Ram, brother, say Ram), singing Manchhi's dirge and dancing. The door-frame was brought near Holi and all the adventurers with panting wiped off their sweat. Then slowly moving the Holi wood back-and-forth, with the force of the log, threw the door-frame into the fire and just then someone—like a backbiting relative of the hunter who brought down the Krauncha bird—must have informed the old lady about this door-frame. Hence, the old lady reached the place where Holi was being burnt, taking long strides with support of her stick and uttering abuses even longer than her steps. Our courageous workers being careful in time moved from the place. And how loudly the old lady was shouting about! After calling out to two or four adults, she got her burning door-frame taken out from the Holi flames and got water sprinkled on it and then with the help of two labourers the old lady took the burnt door-frame back home. We neither said anything nor protested against the old lady. We just kept laughing, pretending to be ignorant, and could not even enjoy the pleasure of getting that door-frame completely burnt, kept taking pity on it.

In our Holi, various kinds of things would be burnt. Some rotten shoes, some torn shirts. Someone's tattered can of forage or someone's broken bamboo basket—whatever came to hand would be throw into the sacred fire of Holi. We used to keep a close watch on the coconuts being thrown into Holi. Where the coconut was lying, when to take it out and after breaking it, how much kernel to give to whom—all this used to be decided with interest and enthusiasm. The whole night we used to sit awake, turning our eyes red in front of the Holi fire, spinning and dancing. Sometimes, we would also sing different types of songs and also used to solve the puzzles. On one hand, there used to be a lot of celebration during Holi in the temple and on the other hand, our mischief outside. Two-three Holi bonfires used to be burnt in the village. We used constantly to be in a competition as to how to make our Holi brighter and keep it burning for a longer period of time. On the second day, Holi would begin becoming calmer and softer, then bringing a kettle of water from our house we would keep it on the burning embers and after the water got hot, we would take bath in the clothes worn before Holi and unconditionally used to carry out the generosity of bathing the nearby appreciative spectators.

Sometimes I feel that by coming closer to dust, water and fire, we reach our true roots. In their presence, some primitiveness within us blossoms like wild flowers. As soon as we saw water, we used to go mad, as if some intoxication was spread in our blood. We used to besmear each other with dust and ash, then pour a bucket of water each on that. Colourless, yet very colourful Holi used to be played among our group.

The second day of Holi, i.e., *padwa* (the first date of lunar-month). In the temple too, *palash* colour would have been prepared and kept ready. Father used to perform the *kirtan*. Colour used to be thrown on Thakurji and later on all those who came for *darshan*. Mukhiyaji used to fill a silver bowl with *roli* and throw it at the devotees who came for *darshan*. On this occasion, we would have had to come dressed in special costumes—dilapidated old dresses—to get coloured properly, and in the direction in which Mukhiyaji used to throw the colour, while we jumping in the middle would get the honour of taking the colour directly on the chest. In case the colour was not easily caught this way, we enjoyed getting drenched in the colour that had fallen on the floor, even by sitting and rolling in it. In this way, along with enjoying the sweet shivering of the body drenched in colours, we would also keep eating the *prasad* of *phagua-lai,* grams and dates.

At that time hardly anyone would have something like a spray-gun. We were almost like 'poor'. The spray-gun made of brass was a very expensive dream. We used to bring empty bottles from home and collect whatever colour was thrown in the temple and fell on the floor and fill it in the bottle. After this, they used to sprinkle colours on each other from those bottles and enjoy the colourfulness of Holi.

The remembrance of Dheraiyas is closely associated with this Holi. Along with Holi, they tie bells around the neck of the bull in the village's outskirt; such sounds of bells and drum-*pipihari* start coming, as if the entire village was dancing with its bells tied. A group of ten-fifteen Bhils of every age used to arrive in the village with variegated costumes. The group used to include not only Bhil beauties with glittering kohl and killer eyes, bulging chests and flowing waves, as if they were beautifully carved from rosewood, but also Bhil youths with ear-length hair, waving wings tucked in red-white handkerchief tied on the head, who had their bodies smeared with ash and their faces painted, and despite being strange, looked charming and capricious. Some old men dressed up like a clown used to play in such a way that people would laugh every now and then. Someone had even a torn, old hat on the head and some had a crown woven from bushes-and-shrubs. Someone used to dance with a basket upside down on his head. In that too, it would have been even more fun when tossing the winnowing-basket or handkerchief with one hand he used to beat the bells in a rhythmic manner, and move around gracefully. We never got tired of seeing the way the Bhil youths and Bhil girls dance freely; yet, we too would have liked to roam around like this being Dheraiya; but our house belonged to a service-class *baniya*. There were no cows or oxen at home. Where would the bells be in the homes?

These Dheraiyas also used to scare me sometimes. Many times, when there was a possibility of fear, I used to prefer to stay at a safe distance from the Dheraiyas and sometimes if a Dheraiya would follow me taking dust in the winnowing-basket to blow it on me, then I used to run home and used to reach the attic window after closing the door. But if I was standing at the window, some mischievous Dheraiya used to take aim at me with bow and arrow in such a way that I would close the window out of fear and then stealthily watch his movements through the crack of the window. When the window was closed, the Dheraiya collecting his bow and arrows used to leave, leaving a trail of hissing footsteps in the dust. The favourite song of these Dheraiyas was, *"Baar baar mahine aaya mota bhai! baar baar mahine aaya re lol! mota aasha rakhiye mota bhai! mota aasha rakhiye re lol!"* (after twelve months, we have come O elder brother! after twelve months, we have com O Lol! we have lots of hopes from the elder brother! we have lots of hopes from Lol!). We used to dance to the sound of the anklet-bells of the Dheraiyas, matching the rhythm with the tinkling bronze-throat of the Bhilnis. Even today, the tinkling of the anklet-bells starts resonating again and again in the brink of the inner most. It comes in a song of Manilal Desai: *"Gaon ke iswan mein ghunghroo bajein, neend se mera sapna jaage, sapna mere balmji ka"* (anklet-bells ring in the outskirt of village, my dream wakes up from sleep, the dream of my beloved). These anklet-bells of the village's outskirt remind me of those days. This was also a dream at that time. Of being a Dheraiya! Anklet-bells be in the legs and waist, around the neck and in the hands. A dandy peacock feather on the head and a *pipihari* in the mouth. A silk handkerchief would flutter in the hand and along with it the winnowing-basket would be jumping in the hands of a charming Bhil girl. Bow and arrow would be hanging on the shoulder and a sword at the waist.

Even today, throughout the lunar-month of Ashadh, an intoxicating sound of youth, bouncing from the banks of green farms, drenches me, and then I feel like throwing away my shoes and socks, burning my chair and table in Holi and setting out somewhere to live forever in the Bhil hut hanging on the waist of the hill. I will sit there with my feet dipped in the waterfall. I will unite my voice with the peacock's cackle. I will tease the cuckoo by speaking its language. If it feels right, brewing toddy I will drink four or five goblets of it and complete the game of this life with fun by eating roots and fruits. I want that white cloud to run its hand through my hair. Let the disposition-cool light of the rainy season irrigate every pore of mine. May the murmur of trees be heard in my heart's instrument and may I come out openly. For enhancing love by drowning the erudition in some eye-tossing blue lotus pond.

But this is not easy. There are no anklet-bells on my foot, a chain tinkles. The curse of civilization, like a snake trapping me in its coils, is hissing. I am also a 'Laocoön'*. It is as though my naturalness has slipped away. I am entangled in the complex mathematics of rule-prohibition that I can

---

* A character mentioned in the Greek and Roman mythology as a seer and a priest, who was killed by two giant sea-serpents along with his two sons.

—Translator

do this and I can't do that. As soon as I think of freeing myself, many strings get pulled. It was only when Nala tore Damayanti's cloth that he could be freed—it seems as if I will have to slash the cloth of my body if I want to be free! That my Holi, those my Dheriyas, that *abeer-gulal* and my world full of *phag*-songs, that *ghonghat* and abuses—I used to like all this, I liked all that very much. Where has all that vanished? What we like, that very thing is the minimum to be had with us? It seems as if I am swimming in some unbearable current, I am helplessly being pulled into the flow of some emotion, my nerves are becoming tight. There is a tingling sensation in the blood. It's like I'm on a potter-wheel. I should stop here now. I feel like closing the windows-and-doors, pulling down all the curtains, hiding myself from top-to-toe under a sheet in complete darkness... but the tension and unrest in the mind is unbearable. How can I convince my mind that is on the potter-wheel? Taking which rosary should I count the beads? In which beads should I bind my mind? I should at least try something, hum...try...!

And...and...everything is now getting heavier-and-heavier while being drenched like wood...some of me comes down after climbing into the air. Like ashes falling on embers, something keeps falling on this personality, keeps becoming cold like ice. The cycle of memory begins to falter. It's as though the wings of imagination never open. Some deep fatigue is loosening all the strings within me. The vibration of the tent collapsing travels through the beads of my spine. I must leave myself, now I must leave my paralyzing words...of mine...!

□

10

'Masanam Margashirshoham!' *(among the lunar-months, I am Margashirsh)* Sri-Krishna had said this in adulthood, after reaching Dwarka; but what he to say at that time when Balkrishna was living in Gokul? Perhaps he would say: 'Masanamhamashvinah' *(among the lunar-months, I am Ashvin)!* Children would love the lunar-month Asvin full of celebrations, wouldn't they? *'Aaso maso sharad poonam ni rat jo! chandaliyo ugyo, re sakhi, mara chowk ma' (*on the full-moon night of Sharad in the lunar-month of Ashvin, O my friend, the moon has grown in my plaza*)*—who will forget this lunar-month of Ashvin immortalised by *garbi*? Navratri and Dussehra, full-moon night of Sharad and Diwali in the lunar-month of Ashvin. Festivals, sheer festivals—having the colour of songs and dances. The earth be flourishing after eating-and-drinking, be fresh—and such fresh life uses to be of the sons of the earth. What is surprising if the clear sky of Ashvin seems bigger and deeper with a little more vividness to the person who sees the murky and pale sky of the lunar-months like Ashadh and Bhadrapad? I also see the moon of Ashvin fresher and more blooming. The greenness of the earth and the coolness of the moonlight seemed to be intertwined in some mysterious way.

Ashvin comes while roaming with *garbhdeep* (lamp in sanctorum). It actually has a close relationship till date with the earthen-lamp. For this, it should also be bestowed with the same extol of *'deepshikha'* (the flame of earthen-lamp) as given to poet Kalidas—*'deep-shikha-Ashvin'* (lunar-month Ashvin as the flame of earthen-lamp)!' During the festival of Navratri, children used to go from house to house asking for *ghee* and oil. We used to go out again on Diwali to beg the donation:

"Aj Diwali, kal Diwali
Parson ko sew Sunwali
Chandamama, ghee dalte ho ya tel?"
(Diwali today, Diwali tomorrow
Attend Sunwali the day after tomorrow
Moon, the maternal uncle! do you pour ghee or oil?)

Can anyone forgo the opportunity of becoming Chandamama by giving *ghee* and oil to these children who came out with the earthen-cup? On one side the light of the moon, and on the other side the light of these earthen-lamps and the earthen-cups—the mind remains drenched with both these lights in such a way that if a little memory creeps in, the rays of that light would shine up even in the darkness.

The dominance of Dussehra was also there in the village just as *mandva* of Navratri. Dussehra ride used to start from our durbar-fort. The ride used to be scheduled to leave at 3-4 o'clock in the afternoon, but preparations would begin in the morning. Bapu had ten to fifteen horses. Those used to be brought to the pond marching through the village. There, careful care of their body and bathing rituals used to take place. Green grass and grains were fed to them. The equipment to be carried on the back of those used also to have to be cleaned. Drops of castor oil used to be poured into the wheels of Bapu's cart. The bull's horn used to be oiled or painted. The rust on weapons like sword, spear, dagger, etc. would have been eliminated. And there used also to be refinement of guns and pistols. Our Bapu's bards used to keep strengthening the tufts of their moustache and also keep polishing their Rajasthani shoes. While they prepared the clean starchy turbans by folding those, someone would get the *salwar* and *sherwani* specially washed and ironed at the washer-man for Dussehra, someone would get the military-suit stitched and someone else would get prepared the royal emblem-drum and stick-flywhisk, etc. Then some used to try to enhance the beauty of their hair and beard with the help of a barber. Not only at the time of Dayamanti's Swayamvar, but also at the time of Dussehra, many people used to get razors while getting their beard, moustache and hair shaved. On the morning of Dussehra, the entire durbar-fort gets dressed up and gets impatient to climb on the sun's chariot and run at a fast pace.

As soon as the morning came, the duet of drums and *tansas* used to start at the door of durbar-fort. We children, moving away from the proximity of sleep, used also to come to the door. During this time someone from the Harijan group would have brought the *heeriya* or *veeriya* battle-horn. When he played the battle-horn with his cheeks puffed out, my feet used to fill with excitement. I used to immediately brush my teeth with the wooden-toothbrush, pour two pots of water here-and-there on the body and chant the mantra like 'Godavari-Kaveri' in hurry. I used to quickly put five to fifteen mouthfuls in my stomach—but all this in the rhythm of that drum. I used to quickly get ready and reach the gate of durbar-fort and start meticulously inspecting the preparations for the Dussehra ride.

I especially used to take a good look at the elder Bapu's white horse. That horse was a giant. What to say about taking care of it that day...! I used to feel, what to say, if God grants the incarnation of such a horse even to me! This was the horse of the elder Bapu; that is why the massage used to be done well to and its bath was also got done with caution. After this, silver anklets used to be tied on its feet And a silver necklace around the neck. A silver harness covering the entire back and bridle used to be provided; and before and after the harness was fitted, its 'trial' used to be done five to fifteen times. Our Miriya, who was taking care of that horse, today his temperament and appearance used to have been different. He used to have worn a washed and ironed military uniform. Khaki cloth turban on the head. Khaki hunting coat with closed neck and shining brass buttons and trousers. Strong knee-length boots with shining leather covers and a wide, strong red leather belt with a buckle at the waist. He used to have hung five-seven silver medals given by the durbar-fort on the occasion of *teej* festival along with the cartridge belt on his chest. Black pointed moustache. Sharp antimony-applied eyes and the stern and restrained face. In that too, when he used to run Bapu's horse, our Miriya was seen and felt only as Mirkhan that day. Five to fifteen times he used to run the horse purposelessly from the gate of durbar-fort to the village, temple and market. He would raise the horse with two legs and rotate it. Sometimes even we children would have the illusion that it is the rider who was more dangerous than the horse. Mirkhan used to crack his whip in the air aimlessly and even in that, when the group of friends of the village would be seeing him, then instead of Bapu's horse, the horse of his mind used to start becoming extremely unruly.

On account of this Dussehra, Babaji of the Ramji temple of our village also used to come. Several exciting legends about him circulated among us. Just looking at Babaji it seemed that his main interest would be in strengthening his body rather than his intellect. One used to feel that he would be more interested in establishing and propagating the importance of his power rather than devotion to Ramji. However, both his memory and intelligence were sharp. And such was his sharp temper, too. When he got angry, he broke the hand of one or two disciples by throwing a loose stick, such things had reached our ears. This Babaji used to keep his underwear and undergarments white. His choice of clothes was something to be admired. Through those clothes, the well-shaped lines of his athletic body used to be attractively visible and yet decorum would be maintained. This Babaji's face was absolutely stunning and it used to look more stunning because of his hair shining with oil and well-maintained matted-hairs. This Babaji was the guru of our durbar sahib, and hence his presence had a definite impact. When he had also joined the Dussehra ride, the splendour of the ride definitely increased.

During this Dussehra, Bapu also used to call one or two bands. Drummers from three or four villages already used to be there. Whenever the band played, our poor rural drum-*pipihari* players would calm down as if they had become pale, just as our village dog would become bewildered and calm down in front of a foreign dog kept by durbar sahib. But later, whenever the rural drum-*pipihari* players got a chance to show their art, they used to risk their lives to play and dance. Among these drummers, Bhirwa Rawaliya of our village was something different. He was such that he could leave even the band-members behind. When wearing woman's {we used to use the word *'randi'* (whore) for this} clothes he would volley an arc of ebullience spinning gracefully in circles in the air on the beat of the drum; that fun was unique. That Bhirwa was a handsome young man. He had great influence in the Dharala-Baraiya community. He used to keep playing drum the whole night without getting tired and would dance with the wedding-guests. The magic of his drum had won the hearts of their wedding-guests. Sometimes, when wearing red handkerchief around the neck, putting the perfume-wet cotton-piece in the ears and chewing betel-leaf in the mouth he used to come out of the market, he would definitely meet some mischievous girl or the other; who would lovingly tell him with her eyes dancing through the veil, "Why Bhirwa-*bhai,* will you eat betel-leaf all alone like this?" And then in the pocket of our Bhirwa-*bhai's* black shirt, in a bundle tied with a string, another betel-leaf used to be definitely present to be given delicately to such a bubbly young lady. This was nothing; what is more, we had become self-appointed witnesses of some of Bheerva-*bhai's* cases of flirting.

Then, if Bapu sahib was in a mood, some firecrackers used to come from Baroda for bursting during the ride on the occasion of Dussehra and at that time I used to pay special attention to follow those who were to burst the firecrackers. I was the offspring of a durbar-official, so if Ram had come into the hearts of those who burst a few firecrackers or *fuljhadis,* those firecrackers used to have come into my hand too and I too would insert the personal programme of bursting those during this ride without the permission of Bapu sahib.

The entire village used to participate in this Dussehra ride. Where the durbar's merchandise was obtained from, that storekeeper used also to be. This storekeeper was like Sudama in appearance. He used to remain wrapped in a wiping-cloth till his knees for all twelve months. If it was very cold or rainy, he used to cover himself with a thick blanket. Actually, he did not have even a single tunic to wear. Whenever necessary, he used to wear the fashionable shirts of his sons and attend the service of Bapu sahib. He was famous for his miserliness, and had no objection or resentment towards it. This storekeeper uncle used to join in this ride by somehow keeping the black cap on his head, which was oily and looked shapeless despite being shaped. This cap of his would have touched the ground four or five times during the ride due to someone's mischief.

How many I have seen every day in a beggar's attire, with open heads or wearing white, black or cashmere caps, they too used to be present today on Dussehra in full Rajputi attire. *Salwar, sherwani* and turban on head. Some poor people used to be absolutely poor, living on the support of the durbar and could barely roll the dice of deposit-and-debt at par. At the time of Dussehra, such people used to wear old shabby but princely style clothes, kept under the rags, and tie a turban of one-or-two *sarees* of their wife on their head, then their attire gave a shocking impression of compulsion, but not of joy—it used to seem so.

When the Dussehra procession was about to come out, some religious rituals would be performed by the royal-priest in the durbar. Sacred verses would be recited. It used to be a sacred remembrance of the campaign that Ramchandraji had started to conquer Ravan. The durbar sahib's stickman used to shout loudly. The bards would recite verses praising the durbar. There used to be gunshots followed by bursts of firecrackers; battle-horn were played and the procession of Dussehra would depart from the main gate of the durbar. At the front, there used to be a durbar-emblem on a bell-ticking camel brought from outside the village. And thereafter the firecrackers. Then the band and the drummers, after those the platoon of horses. This used also to include the horses of the seemly soldiers of the village. After this, if a group of Babas had come to the Ramji-temple, they too would participate in it. Then the leading men of the durbar and village, among them Bapu on the white horse and younger Bapu on several other horses and two-three other elders. After this, carts, *ludhiyas*, etc. Our group used to be everywhere in the ride.

Sometimes, when firecrackers were burst, our group used to be at the front of the ride and when the group of Babas would play the game of Akhara, it used to be in the middle of the ride. When Baba's feat of cutting lemons into pieces with a sword or sleeping on a bed of nails and other such demonstrations took place, we enjoyed watching those; in that too more fun used to feel from finding the lemon slice they had made, cleaning it, placing it in the mouth and sucking it.

Passing through the village this ride used to reach outside the outskirts where there was a Shami-tree *(Prosopis cineraria)*. This tree used to be worshiped there. The offerings used to be distributed. Many people who came in the procession used to pluck a leaf from the Shami-tree and keep it in their pocket. On asking about it, I came to know that it turns into gold. Then someone also explained that if this leaf is preserved carefully then gold can be made from it. After this, without leaving any stone unturned, I plucked a lot of leaves and filled those in my pockets. Kept those with care for months, but apart from the yellowness of dryness, there was no distinctive yellowness, much less the expected golden glow. It felt as if someone had fooled me. Therefore, for the second time when I went to worship the Shami-tree, then while coming back, I also stomped the tree a few times even if whether someone could see or not. It was good that the Shami-tree was not the Ashoka-tree *(Saraca asoca),* my feet were not the feet of Padmini, otherwise only the flowers would have burst due to the blow of the feet, wouldn't they?

On the talk about coming out of this Dussehra ride, it is to mention that Gaekwad Maharaj's colourful Dussehra ride used to be held in Baroda, located thirty-forty miles away from our village—the lucky people who came to see that ride used to talk about that. As if we were watching some magical colourful film, we used to keep seeing the picture of the ride emerging from their eye-witness narration with the eyes of imagination. Durbar sahib also kept silently listening to the talk about the ride to Baroda; but then someone like Mirkhan used to speak out, "Bapu sahib, it is true that gold-and-silver carts, elephants and *ambari,* all these are there. I have turned fifty of my age, but this horse of ours, I have never seen such a horse even in the miles-long ride of Gaikwad Bapu." On hearing this, a light of happiness used to light up on Bapu's face. However, no such boorish fellow was there, otherwise he must have asked that Miriya, "O, you have been serving Bapu's horse here for years, on which Dussehra and in what form did you reach Baroda?"

Even after the completion of this ride, such an atmosphere used to remain in the village for four-five days. Whenever a group of Babas descended on the Ramji-temple, we boys would go to see them. There were twenty to twenty-five Babas in this group. There was no limit to the variety. Bodies smeared with ashes, long matted hair, strangely twisted woods, tongs, sword, spear, axe, lance, trident and many such weapons. Being tied to a tree one or two elephants used to keep swinging in front of their camp; and along with this, the wood of their smouldering fire also used to burn continuously day and night. Some of these Babas used to lie down, some used to sing quatrain, some used to abuse their paternal and maternal uncles, some used to keep sewing their saffron clothes and some used to keep turning beads of the rosary with their fingers. Some used to keep twisting their long, matted hairs after dusting those with ashes, while some would be adjusting the small *rudraksh*-rosary and other rosaries on their body. Someone used to keep decorating his face with ochre-and-sandalwood, while someone extinguishing the fire of smouldering fire with tongs. It was a unique scene. We were both afraid and curious about these Babas. These Babas would capture boys and take them away, an opinion that was also impressed upon us. That is why we all used to meet them with as much caution as possible; certainly not alone.

Whenever I visited this group, I used to spend a good amount of my time in the scientific observation of elephants. How the elephant sits, gets up, how it grabs the smallest thing with its trunk, how it wags its tail and how it eats—I used to watch all this minutely. Had I got proper guidance at the right time after seeing this observation power of mine, I would have been a great zoologist today. But, well, this will not happen in the destiny of Gujarat or India; hence, I became mere the writer of this remembrance. We children used to be very fond of sitting on the elephant and once a Baba even showed the preparation to get me to sit on it, but at that time I was very scared and reluctantly refused.

I say, what kind of fear is this? Like a termite hidden within itself. In which it is sitting, it gnaws at it from within, making it as being left out. Man becomes like rotten wood—he cannot bear any responsibility, any burden, any status. In this way fear is the killer of virility. Many times, the reason behind fear is excessive self-love. Will I have such self-love? Many times, I feel restless, then picking up the letter I do not hesitate to surrender myself to destiny even in the most serious situations. Then I abandon myself in the enthusiasm of 'come what may'. Sometimes, I feel a deep sense of peace in pushing myself the way the wind pushes my boat on the sea. I can sometimes strongly ignore this fear that I will drown, but I cannot easily ignore this fear that someone will drown because of me, and the agony of this very thing makes me more anxious, repels me, as if takes away this precious legacy-like openness. It has happened again and again that despite having the instinct, strength and opportunity to fly, I while flying have fallen mid-air. Some unknown fear suddenly stops my wings. Excessive thoughts, especially fear-induced self-protection, turn as if the speed of the waterfall within me into a canal. How do I get out of this? Even after so many years, its herbs were not found; a lot of knowledge about herbs was found, but what to do with it? Like Sudama's wife, I too have to say: "No interest I do feel in this knowledge, O sage the great!"

□

11

Today I am not in Kanjari, I am in Karnavati-Ahmedabad. Ahmedabad also has a sky above its head, but it is not like Kanjari. The sky of my today is dirty, not as clean as the Yamuna water filled in that Thakurji's silver ewer. It is filled with so many messes and scams inside and outside of me. It is a different thing altogether from that Kanjari's sky.

Whenever a new person entered our village, news of his entry used to spread throughout the village within a moment. Would this not have happened to the sky of our Kanjari, when a new bird came to its shelter? Ever since I started living in Kanjari, I don't remember a single day when my eyes did not have some conversation with the sky. The sky had a lot to say and my eyes too had a lot to hear. If a rainbow has seven colours, the sky has seven hundred colours. The problem is how do I see it? Look at the sky in the morning, look at the afternoon and then look at the evening, look at midnight or look at the dawn. Every moment has its different shades, every moment has its colours. Sometimes, the sky has felt like a Moradabadi plate engraved with enamel in the morning, then it has also felt like a silver plate in the moonlight night. In the summer afternoon, it has also felt like a blazing lead mill. Not only is it fun to see this sky with open eyes, I have tried to taste the pleasure of seeing it even with closed eyes. Sometimes, I have tried to capture the redness of the sun by placing my palm in front of it? Many times, the sky has seemed to me as if it is a reflection of the calm afternoon pond of our village and many times it has seemed sparkling under the cover of the copper-brass pitchers of the female water-carriers. Sometimes there may be some disturbance in the trance mind, in this way I have experienced one or two birds communicating in the sky.

This sky is truly magical realm. It is believed that it also has seven layers—one behind the other, like this. God plays arbitrary and multicoloured games behind these seven layers or curtains. Many times, He topples down, pours, water-gallon after water-gallon, and everything getting drenched in water. Sometimes, taking a golden spray-gun He sprays new-novel colours and everywhere appears the spring of colours. I remember once in my childhood I had gone to Pavagadh with my brother-in-law. Touching the background of the surrounding mountains, a diversity of colours appeared in a limitless expanse. Like a colourful bed of heaven. At that time, I thought again and again, if I get only a single chance to make footprints on this bed...! But my hand was stuck in my brother-in-law's stiffed-hand, like even stronger tea than strong. And his temperament is also such that even if the butterfly of my mind wants to open its wings, it cannot. The misconception that Pavagadh is such a colourful gateway remained true in my enchanted mind for a long time and was later dispelled with difficulty. Has it really gone away?

I don't know why I have some abstruse attraction for the objects and beings moving in the sky. I spent a lot of time catching fireflies flying in the night sky and carrying them in my pocket to scare my friends. I used to just follow the clouds in the sky. I used to run my eyes—better to say, used to take the eyes along—till those disappeared behind some house or bush while floating, just as the string is released in the flight of a kite. I was extremely curious about the new forms that the clouds took every moment. I used to try tirelessly to find the face of some animal, bird or man among the constantly moving lines of clouds and used to involve other companions in such an interesting task.

When the day of eclipse came, I would feel deeply sad. As if an evil mind became active in the manoeuvre to strangle the sky. Nothing in the home used to be touched until the eclipse was over; couldn't even eat or drink. As though we are outcasts from the home! Father, mother, sister etc. all used to sit in the veranda remembering the name of God. Talks about charity and religion would be going on. It used to seem to me that everyone was ready to comply sacrilege when the Sun or the Moon died untimely. I would'nt feel fine at all. We used anxiously to wait for when the eclipse would be over.

But the eclipse would end in its own way and at its own time. What should I do in the meantime? When there been a solar eclipse, the joy of preparing to see it would have been worth it. I used to find a broken mirror from somewhere, fix it, clean it, apply kohl on it. Whenever this was not possible, I used to bring a pot or some such vessel and fill it with water. After that, the programme of observing the eclipse started as soon as it occurred. I anyhow used to observe the eclipse, but my mother, sister and others did not like it. They used to say, "Why is there a need to see a bad thing by taking the initiative yourself?" And if I used to ask how the eclipse was bad, the story of the churning of the ocean used to be told to me in order to clear my curiosity. At a much older age, I could accept the astronomical roles of Rahu (the north lunar node) and Ketu (the south lunar node).

If I find the Ashvin best in the month, then its sky seems best in the Ashvin and the moon is also in the sky. The sky of Ashvin has always seemed to me as lovely and happy as a lake full of lotuses. If you want to say 'satisfied and absorbed in oneself' then you can call it that. Many times, I used to think: "How much fun it would be if I got to roam in this sky!" The birds would jump from one branch to another, from one roof to another, and I used to watch with awe and fascination. These birds seemed more fortunate than me. Neither the imbroglio for doing housework nor the hassle of earning money, they just flew whenever they felt like it, started pecking when they felt like it and sang whenever they felt like it. Neither the hassle of roads nor the worry of a ride. Will we not find any such herbs, by grinding and drinking which we can become light like a balloon and fly as per our wish? I feel like a burden without the sun, without sunlight, without open sunlight. And what the sunflower has, similarly I too have love for the sun; but my partiality, my attachment is only for the moon. Even if the moon were black, I would still love it. There is something in the moon that pulls me from the roots. Perhaps among my three *nadis* (main energy channels)—*ida* (the left channel of energy), *pingala* (the right channel of energy) and *sushumna* (the central channel of energy)—*ida* would be especially strong; I never felt tired while looking at the moon. Is there a rabbit, a deer or an old woman spinning a charkha in the moon, even today, even after spacecraft have landed on the moon, I can't decide. I have considered the moon to be like a silver plate for offerings to God, especially to Balkrishna, and a ball that can be used to play with sticks in Gokul. I categorically deny that it is considered football.

There is a different pleasure in playing and frolicking under the gentle gaze of this moon. If there was moonlight, I used to have enjoyed playing in the dust and sometimes rolling in it. Just as dust gets wet with water, it would also get wet with moonlight. Dust has always seemed different to me in moonlight. The moonlight dust is also different from the sunlight dust.

Be it the lunar month of Ashvin, on it the moon similar to Charudatta's face has risen in the sky, be it an open plaza, in which friends and girlfriends have gathered in groups—only those can know it who have tasted this scene. Is it possible that there is nothing in our blood after looking at the moon? Along with the moonlight, something starts jolting in every heart.

In our Vaishnav Holi, the black figure of Dwarkadhish is seated in a white marble quadrangle, in the soft light of moonlight, amidst white decorations, in a silver bungalow. White cloth, pearl diadem on the head, ornaments also made of pearl, offering of milk and flattened rice in a silver bowl. A mysterious and pure-clean lustring twinkles with glee. There is a glow of moonlight in the atmosphere. Everything is moonlight, cow and Yamuna, *gop* and *gopi*—all of moonlight. The *raas* too, of that very moonlight. Can it ever happen that Nataraja Shankar does not get drenched in these waves of the *raas*? In the dim light of the ghee lamp, in the faint sweet smell of sandalwood, in temple's happily dancing dark-repelling peace, it is as if some deep action of moonlight is being splashed by cramming it up. We all knowingly or unknowingly participate in this process. We used to find ourselves open from within like a lily.

To spend such a full moon night of Sharad, the most suitable place in the home was 'Agashi' (terrace). The name 'Agashi' must not have originated from 'Akashi' (of the sky), right? Just as a house needs a foundation in the earth, it also needs a sky above its head, otherwise the house will become crippled and blind. I was not the resident of such a crippled and blind house. When it rained, I used either to go under the tiled thatch or on the terrace. Be it the moonlight of the lunar month of Chaitra or the moonlight of Sharad, the mind finds satisfaction only in 'Akashpriya Agashi' (Agashi i.e. beloved of the sky). I used to play many games sitting in its lap. *Akka-bakka, iti-kiti, bai-bai chalani, langdi* or something like that. My game used to take place on the terrace. But during festive days, father's blossoms-like fragranced generosity used to tolerate all this. That's why all this game of mine runs smoothly. Meanwhile my sight used also to be there, where a plate filled with milk and flattened rice was kept at a safe place on the terrace to be enjoyed in the moonlight. How could sleep come to my eyes? Antyakshari* and song-*bhajans* used also to go on, small girls also played *garba-raas* and I, the clan-lamp of Hanumanji, used not to miss adding one or two of our glimpses to this *garba-raas* even against their wish. The *garba* used to be perfectly going on till suddenly one of us felt dizzy and fell down. Everyone used to be panic and right then he used to run away, jumping and screaming. Somewhere the Antyakshari would be going on and our companion used to remain at a safe distance and use 'prompting' loudly. Except for some such devilish mischief, our programme on the terrace would have gone on well; and as its delicious ending, the offerings of milk flattened rice were given.

There used to be a method for convalescence of this milk and flattened rice. Krishna had made the mistake of eating Sudama's rough and dry flattened rice in handfuls even though there was cow's milk, I will not do that. Mother used to give me milk and flattened-rice making it as sweet as she wanted to, but I calling it bland would keep getting more sugar added. Then this milk and flattened rice cannot be taken in a leaf-bowl or brass or glass dish? For

---

* A popular verse-competition, in which the first letter should tally with the last letter of a previous participant's verse.

—Translator

this, only a silver bowl is required. In our home, the silver bowl was reserved only for Thakurji, hence I used to have to persuade myself to accept the German silver bowl even if I did not want to. If milk and flattened rice were served in a German silver bowl, I used immediately to put it in my mouth without any delay. That's why my bowl used to remain empty and mother used to get tired of giving milk and flattened rice. At last, the bottom of the bowl used to arrive. Its empty bottom used to sigh in a pitiful tone due to the impact of the spoon and even then, my hunger for milk and flattened rice would keep on flaring in the same way as a blaze flares up due to the burning of *ghee*.

When such a situation arose, even mother used to become a little embarrassed. No matter how much milk and flattened rice that poor lady made, it would be less because of the sweet-loving voracious child like me. Just then 'Gauri' from our neighbourhood used to come running. She used to bring a big bowl full of milk-and-flattened-rice covered by her winsome scarf. Laughing she used to say, "Take it aunty, give it to him." How could that scoundrel lady speak my name? Mother used to think about whether to take milk and flattened rice or not, but Gauri would immediately fill my empty bowl with it. All that happened was that mother's eyes used to become a little moist. There have been many such experiences. There have definitely been some such full moon nights of Sharad, which were more delicious and brighter due to Gauri's milk and flattened rice.

But, on a new moon day, that Gauri too became dear to the Almighty. Such full moon nights of Sharad also came, when mother was there, moon was there, I was there, milk and flattened rice were there but that Gauri was not. The flutter of green scarf of that Gauri, such charming innocent humour, the tapping of her feet—today all this has become only a memory. Gauri acted dishonestly and disrespected me. I had asked in the form of Bhillu, but then she dodged and escaped. She was fun absorber. She might be hidden somewhere behind the face of the moon, behind the curtain of the sky or in my own solitude, silently covering the darkness of some corner of my life. Even if she is not visible, she must be seeing me. Even if she does not speak, she must be listening to me. She must be laughing at this flattery of my writing. But can she leave me completely? I cannot accept it. She must be somewhere within my limits. Perhaps in a new face, in a new form, in a new role. It cannot be said in what guise she would be present and that is why I am handling the front of my remaining life with greater awareness and more consciousness in order to have a sudden sweet argument with her.

□

12

The name of the one whom I consider to be the truth of my sacred solitude, about which I do not like to make any kind of advertisement at all, was announced by me. It is true that whatever resides in the heart will definitely reach the lips in some way. I was not to initiate a talk about 'Gauri', but this secret came out. So now why should I limit this to two-four sentences? A beautiful novella could be written on it, there are so many things. Since the matter has been touched upon here, let me elaborate further.

I believe in rebirth, I believe in the consequences of karma, I believe in debt-contract, because I believe in the continuity of the world and life. A face suddenly flashes, dominates the memory screen and then disappears. After years, it appears again in a different environment or context—in a unique form. What should I call this? What would it be called if two people, who had been living in the neighbourhood for a long time, suddenly meet in a railway compartment after years? The debt-contract itself. My relationship with Gauri is also of debt-contract. When I think of that Gauri today, how do I feel? As if we had been living together for years, in the same house—perhaps in the same lap. One who in case is near, I could say to that even the smallest things of my mind. If I don't do it, there uses to be a burden on my mind. It used to be only me who would basically become restless. You can call Gauri the 'myth' of my life. You can call her my 'daydream'. You can call her the idol of my unfulfilled desires, unfulfilled ideals. Whatever you say, this verily is the reality for me. Today she is not here anywhere in body and yet as long as I am alive, I am not prepared to say 'she's not there'. Her footprints have mingled with my footprints in the dust. Whatever beautiful and variety I see in the marks of my footsteps in the dust (whether you see it or not), I consider Gauri to be the reason behind it. It seems to me that I've walked somewhat being driven by her influence. And that is why without talking about her, my tiny *puran* of this dusty path will seem incomplete to me.

I have a sentimental belief that at the root of motion itself there is an active element like opposition, struggle, pull and tension. To me, at the root of man's motion I seem the magnetic personality of the woman to be the reason, and at the root woman's motion it is the magnetic personality of the woman. I see men and women as the communication centres of positive and negative charges of electricity. Being of both, meeting by being, separation by meeting and meeting by separation—like this, an incident-tradition continues in the form of the action-response and the action-reaction continuously. Man and woman are two powerful incident-elements of a chemical process in the world. Due to this, a complex of changes in worldly dynamics comes into existence on life. Many times, I feel that just like the solar system or the planetary systems, similarly our man-woman systems also have a strange creation dependent on attraction-repulsion. Only divers can attain the essence of this creation, not those eating snail standing on the shore.

I consider Gauri, too, to be the foundation-point of that very above-mentioned creation. A certain charm of her still remains with me, rather I feel it has evolved. Today Gauri is nowhere in the dignity of her body, and yet the childlike innocent counter-relationship that started with her has continued to develop even after her long departure. Better to say that today Gauri has become more mysterious, more comprehensive and subtle. My relationship with her is becoming established invariably more and more in my inner world. Wherever the glimpse of her face has appeared to me, my mind has been entwining there, and from there the silken threads of my poetry have spontaneously emerged. My joy has also evolved from it into a lush green form with delicate colourful wings fluttering.

Perhaps Gauri may not know, along with my development, her development has also been kept going on without hindrance. Since childhood, after walking four or five steps (let alone the whole year with me, she disappeared at some turn of the dusty road, fluttering her wings like a fairy, but after that, laughing and jumping in the new novel form she has been coming at every turn of my path. I had seen her physically in frock and long loose skirt, bodice, scarf. After this, she has given me such adaptability that I can see her in any dress. *Saree* or jeans, braid or lace—all are adorned on her, as if she has a flexible beauty and personality in accordance with whichever country and time.

Today, I feel Gauri living and playing in some way or the other among my relatives and loved ones, and even within me. When she laughs at me, I become ecstatic and when she is sad or blank-mined, I become like a fused lightning bulb. Sometimes this scene uses to be visible in the closed eyes: Gauri is sitting on a long bench in a huge stadium with her lotus-face dipped in her palm, lost in a guilty silence. As soon as I see her like this, I stop standing on the playing pitch. I have a bat in my hand, but it does not rise above the ground. As soon as the ball comes near me, it gets compressed and sits down. I feel the feeling of being out without playing, of losing. Sympathetic friends then also ask, "Why does one become 'mood-less' like this? What has happened?" What should I answer? My answer may perhaps be considered an expression of my sentimentality or madness. Will the essence of my innocent spiritual esoteric relationship with Gauri be truly captured by them? In such a situation, silence seems safe to me. As a batsman putting off his gloves, foot pads, etc., and taking 'early retirement' and comes back to the pavilion, sits on a stool and remains immersed in the depths, similarly, collecting all the senses—eyes, ears, tongue etc.—and shrinking the wings of mind I too have a strong desire to drown somewhere in the recess of a small hollow left. I don't want anyone there, not even my thoughts, to disturb me.

But the strangeness is created there when I try to plant myself in my imperforate solitude, just then a tremor starts under my feet, under my forehead, in my spine. As if Gauri is unable to bear this mental state of mine, she enters my mind like stormy waves from some empty space. She pulls back all my covers, flips all my off switches and illuminates my solitude. I feel a sweet tickling sensation. Like a burnt crust sticking to the bottom of a pot is scraped off with a rolling pin, in this way she keeps scraping off many of my scabs with her sweet and sharp gaze. As if I attain *kayakalp* (transformation by body)—*manahkalp* (transformation by mental state). My hands start feeling energetic again. Taking the bat again I go to the field, and start the unfinished game. Gauri is sitting there in the pavilion counting each and every run of mine, and I feel happy. My hands and legs get tired, but I don't even want to leave the playground. Finally, the descent of darkness begins, Gauri leaves all thoughts and runs into the playground, snatches the bat from my hand and I, throwing the ball with my hot hand, step following her towards the pavilion.

Gauri has been my best well-wisher. I remember the plum incident. Gauri liked plums very much. She used to tell me, "There are very nice plums on the bank of that pond." And immediately, I used to understand the meaning of this. In the evening, I used to make all the pockets of my shorts-and-shirt empty in front of her feet. Smooth, shining plums. Just what was left that I used not to bring those after tasting them like Shabari. Gauri used to take the plums, taste those, and her eyes would sparkle with joy and immediately I would start chirping remembering its taste, as if the plums uses not burst to even a thorny tree like me. Once upon a time, while tasting the plum, her eyes fell on my hand. There were red marks of thorns here and there on my hand. Then Gauri thoroughly examined me. Where there were scratches on my hands and legs—she looked at it closely; and then Gauri never let me go to pick plums. If I wanted plums, she would bring a cup of rice from home used to get those for me from the plum-seller in barter—and that too in such artistic way that the family members of neither mine nor hers could know about this.

Gauri would be happy if I got good marks in the exams. If she could, she even used to make vows of small offers. Once when I had fever, she worshiped *tulsi* for a week and that too without any noise. Whenever there was a debate or factionalism among equal friends, Gauri's opinion used always to be in my favour. Sometimes Gauri would even go to scold others for my sake and once even her mother had said, "Why are you being mean for that Bhagat Kaka's son? Why to arbitrate for others unnecessarily?" Then... then "Where is the arbitration for others?"—saying this she calmed down. Had Gauri's brother not told me this, I would never have been able to know from Gauri's mouth.

Gauri was one or two years older than me. Round face,

delicate structure. Smooth, somewhat wheatish colour, delicate nose. Eyes very clean and transparent. There was something in it due to which hardly anyone used to feel emotionless towards her or feel like displeasing her. She was eager to do everyone's work. She didn't say anything for herself. But in case she felt injustice or perceived a lie, she would definitely have fought. She did not recognise fear. Her maturity or wisdom seemed quite high for her age. I don't know why, but she felt most comfortable with me. I too did not feel good on the days I did not see her or did not meet her; that day seemed miserable. Once she went to another village with her aunt for ten-fifteen days, during those days I felt as if I was alone in a family full of people. When that Gauri left forever, I don't have the courage or preparation to calculate how much of mine she took with her and how much of mine was left here.

I had a different kind of world with this Gauri; of course, of the childhood—of the games. Gauri had sole rule in that world. Whatever game was decided by Gauri, she would get it played. Whatever work she assigned to me, I had to do. We used to spend hours playing the game of house-house in the backyard of my house, behind the partition of the cot. Only I used to act in role of a *seth*. Starting from a merchant, a courtier, a chief, a blacksmith, a carpenter, a tailor, a barber, a potter, a drummer or a beggar, I have enacted different characters with great success. We also took advantage of the lessons taught in school through sports. Once Gauri became both Suniti and Suruchi and made me Dhruv. That day, that scoundrel girl had taken my breath away by making me stand on one leg. For the second time, the game of Swayamvar of Prithviraj and Sanyukta started. At that time Gauri was Sanyukta, I playing Prithviraj. Prithviraj was to kidnap Sanyukta by picking up her with both his hands—this was her insistence. (She must have seen it in a drama or

Ramlila somewhere.) I had to do that heavy work and then she laughed out loud...! Once we started the game of the great renunciation of Buddha. She became Yashodhara and asked me to become Buddha; and along with this, she also kept giving me detailed information about how to enact the great renunciation. If I am Krishna then she is Radha Gori, if I am the groom then she is the bride—this 'goes without saying!'—Like this, we must have played many times. If I became a cowherd, she would milk the cow, if I ploughed the farm, she would bring breakfast, if I went to earn, she would cook food—we used to play like this again and again. Once, I remember, I came home after earning from office. Gauri served the plate. She started saying to me, "Take this thick *tikkad*." I said, "Why did you cook this thick *tikkad*? I want chapatti." Gauri said, "There is no wheat at home, how can I cook chapatti?" Throwing up the stool, I got up angrily. Wearing a cap made from a bag on my head, and putting on a coat I started walking. Gauri came running. Holding my hand she said, "Sit, sit, I swear! You take Thakurji's *prasad* along with *tikkad*." And I became calm. Ate and then lay down for a bit. In this game, the *tikkad* was made from a large round potsherd and in case the chapatti had been cooked, it would have also been made from a round potsherd; I should clarify this. Many times, the afternoon snack was also used artistically in the house-house game. Many times, a temple would also appear in our game. I used to bring two empty boxes and make a drum out of those and play it. Like my father, I used to sing *kirtan* and Gauri used to take up the tune while playing cymbal. Once the *kirtan* was going on perfectly. I and Gauri were engrossed in it, when I don't know what occurred to me, in the manner in which my father used to address my mother, I said to Gauri, "Jamu, bring some water, my throat is dry." And as soon as Gauri stood up to bring water, she looked back and saw my mother standing there. That day my mother also said, "What do these foolish children do?" While saying she laughed in such way... then this whole story had become a source of *'Brahmanand-sahodar-anand'* (the joy as if the sibling of divine bliss) for the family-members. That day Gauri bowed down in shame so as not to ask the question. Even today, when I see red juicy mulberries, I remember that bashful Gauri. Even in her soft voice, her shyness was revealed in an extraordinary way.

Sometimes this Gauri used to become *gopi* and churn curd at home. We, Krishna and cowboys, used to enter her home. Used to loot butter. Some friends along with me would scream sounding *'khon-khon'* and jump like monkeys. We used to make a lot of noise. The elders in the nearby houses used to be disturbed during their sweet afternoon sleep and they would threaten us. We all used to run away. In case Gauri had wore the scarf-*saree,* its edges being unknotted used to be besmeared in the dust. My *pancha* used to slip from my waist and we would hardly reach safe—'no man's land'—in a lot of perplexity while trying to maintain the honour of Gopi-Krishna in attempt of Panchali manner.

It is difficult to say what could not be included in this house-house game of ours. Whatever incidents of school or durbar, temple or market, drama or Ramlila, village or city, heard or read, reached us. Those were transformed in a big way into this house-house game of ours. Gokul and Vrindavan, Baroda and Mumbai were not distant places for our games. In this game, it was not at all difficult to become a peacock and a peahen, a horse, a donkey and an elephant, a cock and a cuckoo. Who knows how many times we would be born and die in this game. Becoming a father, becoming a grandfather, becoming a guru and becoming a Maharaj—all this was very easy for us. Gauri, too, had become a mother and grandmother. Many times, a boy was born to her and she died. Many times, I had to perform the last rites of a dead boy. I didn't know that the rituals we used to do in the game would have to be performed seriously by the elders for Gauri. Gauri died—I saw her die with my own eyes and yet I don't know why I keep feeling that she is still alive. Even today, I have not been able to forget the shining eyes with which Gauri welcomed my arrival from her deathbed. I can't forget her easy sweetness and simple smile.

Today I see in front of my eyes, an embroidered dice-board is spread. The gold pieces are placed exactly opposite to each other. A comfortable seat is also ready for the companion to sit in front. Ivory dice is also ready. But where is the one to throw it; where is my childhood friend's delicate hand tinkling with the bell-bracelet of gold? It seems as if I have been sitting in front of dice-board for years. With the hope that once, just once, she will come here as a true reflection of my faith. At least I will not have to play the last gamble of life alone; Gauri will be included in this. I can't say in which guise and in which form this Gauri will appear; it is also possible that that innocent tiny wise girl may come in the form of some currency or ring, some illusion or shadow, to play the final game grandly. I have to keep the post of my eyes and ears continuously alert and wait for her while being awake. That wise girl coming should not feel that I have been careless about her even for a moment. Can I be a little careless about Gauri? What will that Nand Samvedi* say to me if I stay so?

□

---

* This is one of the pen-names of Chandrakant Sheth, the author of this book; his other pen-names are *Aryaputra, Daksh Prajapati,* and *Baalchandra.* However, also a collection of some essays written by him has been published under the title 'Nand Samvedi'.

—Translator

13

Actually, I was to reach Diwali as soon as possible after the full-moon day of Sharad, but Gauri came in between and came with authority and I had to step into my inner-most with her; but Gauri, that *'Sancharini-Deepshikha'* (the lamp-flame having a transmissible attribute) had the opportunity to twinkle for a very short time on my dusty path. Remembering the gentle light of that lamp, let us enter into the dazzling light of the festival of lamps. In fact, I used to start feeling the touch of its light only from the full-moon day of Sharad. I used to measure every day how much distance had decreased from the full-moon day of Sharad to Diwali and was thrilled with the thought of celebrating it grandly.

Diwali has the lighting of *deepmala* (garland of lamps) and also the sound of fireworks. Whenever I remember Diwali, I remember 'Malaye Bhillapurandhri'. I also remember that 'Bhiladi' Sati who had wavered even the ascetic Shankar. If the full-moon day of Sharad is Ganges, then Diwali is Yamuna. Many times, Diwali is visible to me in the form of Yamunaji. A beautiful shapely statue made of black marble, in whose palm a golden lamp-flame shines—that very goddess is *deepotsavi* the lamp-festive!

All of us—brothers, sisters and friends—used to start dreaming of Diwali from the full-moon day of Sharad itself. In the dream, mountains of sweets used to be visible,

Annakoot used to be visible and the colourful royal fun of the sparkle and thunder of fireworks also used to be kept weaving into it. I used to plan in detail what kind of firecrackers I would bring in this Diwali and how many crackers I would burst at which places. I used to have perhaps more interest in it than the Finance Minister would have been in the preparation of the budget. I kept asking my mother again and again to give me more crackers this time. Mother used to be frustrated with this leech-style questioning and would sometimes say irritably, "Rubbish, keep watching at least? Let Thakurji burst the crackers first, do you want to burst those before even He does?"

If some good fruits or some beautiful thing comes to our home and if the mother talks about Thakurji, we all used to become completely silent. It used first to be offered to Thakurji, and only later would be given to us. Even if firecrackers were brought into the home, Thakurji's share used to be separated first and we used to get the rest only.

Our Thakurji was an honourable member of the family. We—three brothers—and as if He the fourth, the adopted one. In every matter His first right was Omni-accepted. When we used to feel cold, Thakurji too felt cold. If we used to feel humid, He also felt humid. If we used to like bursting firecrackers, then how couldn't He like it? Like us, the mother also took interest in pampering Him with Yashoda-feeling. That's why sometimes I used to feel jealous—envy—of Thakurji and yet the atmosphere at home or the rules of the home were such that we could only escape Thakurji's rage by accepting it without any argument.

Only after Thakurji's share in the firecrackers was separated, the shares of us brothers and sisters used to be separated. Father did not have the ability to spend much money on crackers. Hardly ten to fifteen rupees used to be made available for crackers. Thakurji used to take away the first part and the rest was taken by all of us, the general public. Used to take even the *tikdi* and *phuljhadi* by having counted. The interest, acumen and alertness that we had in the distribution of firecrackers at that time, we did not maintain the same later even when the property was divided among us brothers. I used to inspect the crackers given to me very closely. After this, keeping all the firecrackers well, I used to make a systematic arrangement in my mind as to when and what to burst. If such alertness would have been maintained everywhere in life, then... but alas! This golden quality of alertness never entered my mind. Didn't ever know how to tie this bundle of the five basic elements neatly in the classical discipline! Now bear the game of karma... wander around making footprints on the dusty path!

There used to be ten days left for Diwali, since then all of us friends used to organise a summit every night. I used to do this with my childhood friends, *"Aj Diwali, kal Diwali; parson ko sew Sunwali"* (Diwali today, Diwali tomorrow; attend Sunwali the day after tomorrow), but apart from this, used to make sure that which *phuljhadi,* which firecracker or which *anaar* would be burst by the lamp of which house, from which door of the house. Then, for bursting, there was also the task of collecting sulphur from matchsticks. It was also a duty to search out the old tablet-bursting revolver kept safely in a box or shell or the storehouse, remove the rust from it and pour oil in the spring and trigger. Apart from this, the responsibility of finding the crackers and hiding those in a safe place was not as simple as eating vegetables. We friends used to make a lot of efforts to ensure that this work goes smoothly and gets complete success in it.

Then there was the problem of breakfast along with crackers. It was also decided which breakfast to bring from home on which day and in what quantity. In order to ensure that we younger friends lest do anything wrong in this delicate matter, our elder friends used to have to take this responsibility. I remember that these our elder friends, inspired by their altruistic mind, themselves used to start bursting in good faith such risky and deadly 'items' in good faith so that we should not cause unnecessary harm to ourselves due to the dangerous firecrackers like atom-bombs, aeroplanes, big firecrackers, big *anaars*, etc. Then, even at breakfast, we younger ones lest spoil the fun-filled atmosphere of Diwali by fighting with inner jealousy unnecessarily—with this auspicious thought, the pain or toil that a charitable monkey had to endure for two cats, the same our elder friends too used to do with a smile.

On the day of Diwali i.e., a holiday. Days of eating instead of studying. The hunger for the *shat-ras* (six flavours) used to more easily arouse than for the *nav-ras* (nine emotions). In case *papad,* nugget, rice-*papad,* gram-noodles etc., were kept somewhere in the street, in the premise or in the courtyard to dry, then I used to keep putting a little of it in the mouth as *prasad*. Those days, I used to be completely alert with our sense of smell as to whose kitchen was smelling which dish. With more special efficiency than the officials of the L.I.B., I used to collect even the smallest information about which dish has been made at whose place, which one is being made or is about to be made, and used to think of an effective strategy that to whose house I should go in my personal capacity and to whose house friends should be taken as a community.

Once in our locality, the sweet smell of something being fried in ghee came from Ganga aunt's kitchen. My mind was also like that *laddu*-glutton clown. The tongue was not under its control, the mind was wandering. Therefore, out of compulsion, we got up and entered Ganga aunt's home with humility. One of us was a witty boy. He started saying,

"Ganga aunty, tell me, are you frying *gujiyas*?" "Yes bro! During this Diwali," she said, showing me, "When his father comes home, something should be available to be catered in the plate, right?" I said, "But aunty, where does my father eat anything from outside?" Aunt started saying, "O fool, can one call it something from outside? I have cooked it from pure milk and that too with my Vaishnav hands. I don't keep anything like *chhutihar* (enough for untouchability)." My friend started saying, "Hey aunt, your *gujiyas* use to be cooked very good, Radha aunty, Shardia and Kashi aunty all say this. They also say that your fresh *gujiya* is a different thing." "It's so, bro, eat it now, eat it after five days, it will make a difference, won't it?" "Difference will have to, that's what I was saying to him." I said, "This time we are to eat only freshly fried *gujas (gujiyas)* at Ganga aunt's place, if this happens then we will not eat it during Diwali." Ganga aunt started saying, "Why is this so? What will be lost by eating five-seven *gujas*? Here, these *gujas* are hot, take these at a distance. Eat these, when these cool down a bit."

And this is how we became *ghuguriya* that day by eating *'ghuguri' (gujas)*. Such our group used to roam from one house to another every day, trying out strange tricks.

This Diwali festival had a different glory in our home. Worship of Thakurji would be done at home. Used to perform Annakoot on New Year's day. Intensive preparations for this used to go on under father's supervision. The millstone used to keep on singing and echoing again and again. The pestle used to keep jumping in the mortar, the sieve kept moving in someone's hand and the winnowing-basket keep chaffing its wings. Sometimes plates used also to go round to glean the wheat. Everyone in the home, elder-or-younger, used to get work as per their capacity. Mother, father and elder sister used to take bath for servicing Thakurji. Many types of dishes used to be prepared—*dhor, mathadi, guja,* *dhari, chandrakala, jalebi, barfi, peda, laddus* of pulses and *chashma, churi, mohanthal, laddus* of lentils, *mung, urad and bundi, sakkarpara, manbhog* etc. The edible things like *thor,* which could last for a long time, used to be prepared first. And things like typical *manbhog* used to be prepared on the last day. Along with these, nugget, *papad, mathiya, suhari noodle*, etc. made of various pulses used also to be fried; various types of *saag, raita, bhajiya, bada* etc. used also to be prepared. Our Thakurji belonged to 'Anasakhadi'*; hence, instead of rice, father used to keep a pile of *kheel* and on the morning of 'New Year' the worship-room used to be filled with Annakoot. That day mother and father used to remain awake the whole night. I used to wake up early in the morning. By the time father offered Annakoot, my aim used to take bath and get ready as quickly as possible.

Father would pick up Thakurji and His means and materials and mother would take out the fraction from all the Annakoot, and only then we would have had the right to touch the Annakoot. Where in the Annakoot was the edible thing that I liked, I used to have seen it in advance on the pretext of visiting Thakurji, hence, as soon as I entered Annakoot, the relishing duet of hands and mouth would have begun. Mother used to interrupt me in between, but then all the senses except the sense of taste used to become almost unconscious. After Annakoot was over, father would lovingly reach all the Vaishnav houses in the entire village with the *prasad* packed in packets. This custom was maintained as long as we lived in Kanjari. If this Annakoot was completed without any hindrance, then there used to be no limit to the joy of mother and father.

In the meantime, due to the majesty of Annakoot, my respect among my friends used to suddenly increase. The

---

* In Vaishnav religion, where dishes are prepared in milk instead of water. That Thakurji is called Anasakhadi.

laddu of *prasad* used to have been useful in solving many questions troubling me. I used to be able to attract two or four jealous friends to my side by luring them with *prasad,* but for some unknown reason, my self-respecting instinct did not seem very appealing to me. Even today, I have deep dislike for the relationship based on greed and fear. I know that this unpleasant thing uses to be practiced by me everywhere even unwillingly, but how can I get happiness with it?

On the day of Annakoot, a special programme of Govardhan Puja used also to be celebrated. Under the guidance of my father, all of us friends used to make the structure of *Govardhangiri* (hill of Govardhan) by bringing big stones, cow-dung, branches, leaves, etc. My intelligence would be praised in such programmes. Later, after coming to Ahmedabad, I also took great interest in explaining 'Maholla Mata' (Mother Malla). Nowadays, I have suppressed many such interests out of little consideration of my elderly stature; it is not wrong to say so. However, these interests are not dead yet. Rather, my present role makes me uneasy from top to toe when these become alive.

On this Diwali, Lakshmi-puja, Sharda-puja used to take place, but in our Pushtimargiya-home (the home following the norms set in Pushtimarg sect of Vaishnavism), all this used to be included in the worship of Thakurji. They used to have no separate glory. Sharda (an epithet of goddess Saraswati) resides on the tongue of our Thakur and Lakshmi resides near His feet. Despite this, I used to feel good to roam around in durbar-fort wearing newly ironed clothes on such occasions of worship. Wearing the clothes looking like foreigners in the dust of the village, I used to move with pride from one temple to another, from another to the third—this way in the 'New Year'. Sometimes, I used to make others overawed by wearing transparent coloured paper spectacles costing two or four *annas*. While doing this, whichever temple I visited, I used also to do comparative study of the Annakoot and used to be proud of the superiority of the Annakoot of the Vaishnav temple.

This Diwali, I am a witness to the way that some poor or infamous slum dwellers used to hover about our place for 'packed *prasad*'. Father never avoided people who came to the house asking for anything, absolutely not at least for *prasad*. Father used to go informing mother about giving the *prasad* and mother used to give a little *prasad* while grumbling at the people who came to ask for it. On the one hand, the *prasad*-loving face of us used to be reflecting in her mind and on the other hand, the Vaishnavism inherent in distributing *prasad* generously and the insistence to distribute it to everyone without any hesitation was also there. I understood this position of my mother and that is why I could never call my mother stingy or non-munificent. She could not come out of the compulsion of the situation, due to some weaknesses and today I too am carrying the legacy of the same weakness suffering here-and-there mainly because of my own self.

Whenever I see poor children searching for unexploded firecrackers, *phuljhadis* etc., in the dust of the road during Diwali, my poverty causes unbearable pain to me. A kind of bitterness towards this life and the world—towards myself too—spreads in my mouth. At such times, I feel as if I have committed some crime in celebrating Diwali. Despite this, I did not distribute the firecrackers I had bought for my children among the poor; or I did not give up the pleasure of eating anything sweet. This 'contradiction' of mine makes me restless, always keeps me in tension and even though the solution to get rid of it was at hand I use to write on paper with humidity about the oddity of not being able to do it in life. What should I call this? Sometimes I really feel that one or two firecrackers should explode in such a way that my hollowed being would be shattered to pieces and if there was any light left inside, it would be free by being applied into those unfortunate blind eyes. I don't know how far away such a Diwali of good fortune will be, but deep in my heart I feel the need for such a Diwali intensely. Especially in today's cold winds.

□

14

In the cold of winter, I have been getting the taste not of cruelty but only of sweetness. Early in the morning, the question of taking out the five basic-elements from the quilt would arise, then I wouldn't know how many hot abuses I used to give to chill, but the chill used to remain pink and smile sweetly and fresh on the soft cheeks of a child. The chill is a paronomasia of the affection and the power. How even the sun-like sun becomes as soft as butter! When coconut oil was being used to be rubbed on my body, I feel as if incense is also rubbed on me along with it. Wouldn't the idea of applying turmeric paste come to one after seeing the sunlight? Perhaps it is because of the aura of winter that the warmth of Holi in the lunar month Phagun seems to me as intoxicating and delicious as the mango blossom.

I have seen winter blossoming in sixteen *kalaas* (divine qualities) in the red cheeks of children and in the white-skinned cheeks of a Kashmiri girl. I observe its innovation not only in the redness of a ripe tomato but also in the dark glow of an ugly brinjal. This winter rattles the teeth of the mouth, tells that steam is coming out of mouth in the form of a sigh, it passes through my body like a 'torpedo', sending shivers down my spine, and yet I find its embrace exhilarating. It seems as if the space around me was shimmering in the light of the beautiful and happy face of the earth with lush green and rich in crop. There is such beauty which blooms with the cold and spreads within—in the form of the fragrance of *hemant* (pre-winter season), in the form of the power of *shishir* (winter). Every winter, the sun of the new year—the sun of *hemant*—opens before me with the refreshing flavour of hope and enthusiasm. In this, not only mine, but the thrill of some unique poem of the whole world, gets excited in such a way that redness is issued forth on a healthy face.

Even when it is winter in the city, it feels good; but there is something unique about a rustic winter. In winter, when I see a ragged child sleeping on a cold sidewalk spread with a newspaper in the city, I get frightened by the feeling of some chilled cruelty of my own. I find this winter cold to be a more severe shock than lightning. My mind wishes: is it not possible that from one of my blankets not nine hundred and ninety-nine, but nine hundred lakh blankets can be born? But it seems as if I have lost both Draupadi's truth and Krishna's compassion in some gambling. I have emptiness and am sitting like an ostrich with my mind and eyes fixed on the dust of the earth with my eyes closed—while remembering this, I perform the alchemy of ending the extension of my life too like the days of winter. But this is an escape, this also is a madness, but I have come to like it. I feel happy in my heart with a feeling of being blessed to have established an infamous(?) colony with the help of memory where there is no one else. This is also a *leela,* which has been born out of the will to live.

In winter there is complete silence in the village till eight-nine o'clock in the evening. The village-floor as quiet as the village pond! If a vehicle passed through the village at untimely hours, it used to have created a rattling stone in the peace. That's all. As soon as winter came, we used to take out blankets and sheets. In order to bask in the fire, we used to take out the clay-hearth, made by mother months ago, from the attic. This hearth used to be kept in the middle of the hallway of the home, as though rostrum had been placed in the canopy. Patches were burnt in that hearth and the eyes used to be filled with smoke-and-tears. We used to blow and remove the veil from the eyelids of the sleeping fire. If necessary, we used to add *raintha* and *fatwari* too. When the fire used to conflagrate perfectly—as a volcano—then we used to warm our palms, soles, back, etc., with this fire; as if the red light of the hearth-deity was inciting the glory of the copper-age culture on all the faces nearby. I used to remember our Bhil hero brothers! I would remember our ancestors of that stone age. The secret of the discovery of fire used to start shining softly on the mind from some inner spark. The feeling of *'namiye agankool'** is more evident in this type of environment.

Completely different from the scary stove of Baliyakaka, a unique sheet of world and religion was woven around this mother's warm chest-like winter hearth. *Chaurasi Vaishnavon ki varta,* (talks of eighty-four Vaishnavs), *Do sau bavan Vaishnavon ki katha* (stories of two hundred and fifty-two Vaishnavs), *Harirayji ka shikshapatra* (Harirayji's teachings), *Srimadbhagwat, Nitya-niyam ki kathaen* (stories about routine-rules' observation)—from all these, something or the other used to be made available for hearing. At that time father was the centre of this night meeting. He used to remain drenched in the essence of *satsang* and make everyone drenched. Sometimes he used feel like being in trance, then he used to sing in a loud voice: *"Dridh in charanan kairo bharoso, dridh in charanan kairo..."* (keep firm trust in these feet, firmly in these feet...). Mother and sisters all used to sing. Sister used to sing the verses of Dayaram with very beautiful melody. Mother had barely

* Gujarati-language poet Rajendra Shah's line 'Agniphal ko vandan' (salute to Agniphal).

studied till fourth grade. I used to enjoy a lot when she recited the corrupted versions of Sanskrit compositions like the best *stotras* (hymns) or Yamunashtak or Gopigeet. Sometimes I even used to tease her. Then she used to say laughingly, "Stop, rascal!" Saying this, she used to run to hit me, then teasing her by showing thumb I used to run away from her at a fast pace. When such incidents used to start breaking the decorum, father's Hitler-like orders interfered and it used to seem as if everything was locked in a box after having been folded and kept.

More result-giving and history-making assembly than the meeting held near this hearth used to be held outside the house, near the bonfire. Most of the time, the special possibility of such assemblies used to be in the playground of the unclaimed school. Around seven-eight o'clock, after crossing the boundary wall of the school, our playful group used to enter its playground with authority; we used to ignite the dry branches-leaves of tree, papers, garbage etc. those were available there. Sometimes fuel obtained from here-and-there through the art-of-smuggling used also to be useful. When the flames of the bonfire started touching our heads, we used to jump with joy. Around it, friends used to play *raas,* drama, dance, talk, abuse, Antyakshari and sometimes even fight. This bonfire creation was truly a *'navaras ruchirahyadaikamayi srishti'* (a creation of interesting joy full of nine emotions). Even today, I feel a great dilemma in deciding whether that creation was excellent or the poetic creation. Call it bonfire-deity (*alaav-dev* or *alaaviya-dev*), the questions of how many books used to have been solved in front of it; whether that Baba has controlled that widow Rama or not, for whom has that sorcerer-exorcist practiced black-magic, with whom does that lady-barber Savli sleep these days, where does that *paan*-seller Manu pry these days, that how much Veerji

Thakkar has staked in betting, how much did that Shania lose in the teen-patti game of playing-cards yesterday, why doesn't that Shambhu Maharaj have children—such things, perhaps too flamboyant and big for our age, used to be presented in this meeting with full spice, in pictorial form and sometimes with acting. Not nine, rather nine hundred and ninety-nine pots of flavours used to be poured out here with godly generosity. Keep drinking sip after sip, palm-cup after palm-cup. In this group, all kinds of vegetarian and non-vegetarian things used to be served. Sometimes these meetings used to become a springboard for serious disputes among the elders. In these bad times, the Section-144 used to be strictly imposed against such meetings. But despite this, like the secret meetings of Christian people, these meetings used to be organised in someone's yard, in someone's pasture, sometimes at the gate of Mahadev temple or in the porch of an empty house. The day we were unable to attend these meetings, it used to as if we have missed living that day.

Just like the experience of the winter night, the experience of the morning was also very exciting for me. When I used to participate in the tonic programme for going out in the morning, it was not only a special but a happy request from the people at home. My body was like a cockroach or an ant. Mother was always worried about me. Therefore, generally she used to cooperate in making my body tight. In the morning, wrapped in a quilted cotton-jacket and a two-patched blanket, I used to go out wearing a pair of rustic shoes with a creaking sound like wooden-slippers, bought from Mathura for my elder brother but later reached me when fell short in size. Its éclat used to look as if our troop was going on an adventurous trip to the North Pole. Our troop used to march through rough, agricultural, dusty roads. There used to be sticks in hands made of tree branches cut here-and-there. Some even used to have a torch. While passing through the village, we used to keep throwing the torchlight here-and-there as if would be winking at the open ventilator-and-window of someone's house, and used also to keep hearing abuses as heavy as delicious dishes. Sometimes we used to throw the torchlight two or four times into the high sky to brighten the face of moon who was looking dim. The wooden toothbrushes used to be prepared by cutting a branch of any acacia or *karanj* coming on the way and a competition would begin as to who could quickly make that toothbrush smaller than the little finger by chewing it. Then sometimes on the way, there used to keep going on mysterious discussions about ghosts, demons, jinn, *brahm-rakshas*, etc. The most minute information used to be given about on which tree the ghost resides, nearby which grave the jinn dwells and on which way the witch keeps wandering. It would be such subtle information that if you sent a letter to them even without a postman, it would automatically reach the designated ghost's destination. Some boys' hearts used to feel nervous on hearing this, but the warmth of each other was such that the fear used only to keep whirling around us the way the *kaliyug* goes round outside the city of king Nal—but as soon as we entered inside, it was as though it itself used to experience some fear.

Travelling through rough roads our troop reached the flag station of Kanjari. This was a metre-gauge railway-station on the railway-lines from Champaner Road to Pavagadh. Hardly anyone would be getting down or boarding at this station. All transportation transactions used to take place through Halol. After reaching the station, we used to listen to the tracks to determine whether the train was coming or not and when the train was about to come, we used to raise our hands to signal to stand still and if it remained standing, we would immediately run away.

Once I had a *duanni* (two *annas*) of brass given to me by my mother in my pocket. Friends forcibly took it from me and kept it on the railway-track. The train came and passed through that *duanni* safely. But my *duanni* became flat. As soon as I saw this, my face also became like that of *duanni*. There was only one worry in my mind, what would I tell about this *duanni* at home? That day the entire route became tasteless to me. Went home, mother asked for *duanni* back, but that was not able to be used as a coin. She fretted. Scolded the boys who used to take me for walks. As a result, I was ostracised from that circle of friends. Those days were very humiliating for me. I used to wake up in the morning, go out of the home, keep seeing those friends without inviting and something used to start happening to me. This chilled cruelty of my friends was burning me in the winter. Ultimately, to resolve this boycott, I had to take refuge in the God's *prasad*. For a few days, I voluntarily gave up my share of *laddus* and dedicated its valuable accumulation like a Khandiya king to the lotus-hands of the friend-circle and due to the *prasad* of the God, the dawn of happiness again appeared in the entire friend-circle. My coronation was done again with a festive-love in the group of friends.

I also remember those winter days when I was involved in the newly started trend of gym in our village. Used to sing the national anthem. Used to bow my head in front of the picture of Bajrangbali and then perform exercises like sit-ups, push-ups, etc. I could never be a firm practitioner in this gym-trend. The Malkham move was not even possible. As soon as I entered wrestling, I used to fall flat on back. Be it any game, except the game of *geldi,* I used to have been caught. My credibility of the subsist gazing was enough in that. It used to be fun while exercising in this gym, even more fun used to be eating *laddus* filled with dry-fruits at home after exercising. Instead of throwing a ball in the gym, I used to have found it more enjoyable to slowly put the *laddus* filled with dry-fruits, bit by bit, into the stomach with sweet sunlight and in a gentle motion. In the gym-trend, I used to have remained neutral, standing on the sidelines. What story to be told about how and how many thorns of neutrality have been pricked at good-and-bad times? For right now, only this I can tell that this my *sri-ang* (body) is incubated by many winters.

□

15

The *Ritu Samhar* of the poet Kalidas begins with the hot-season—with the summer. And what kind of heat?

'Prachanda suryah sprihaniya chandramah
sadavagahakshavarisanchayah dinantarabhyah
abhyushantamanmathah'

(with its intensely burning sun, with its favourable moon, with its reservoirs of water for frequent bathing, the season which is pleasant at the close of the day, and in which the Cupid becomes very much tranquilised)—even if we leave aside the matter of such Cupid (Manmath, i.e., Kamdev, the deity of love), my childhood can definitely give proof of the correctness and appropriateness of the other four composite adjectives. *'Phani mayurasya tale nishidati'* (the snake takes refuge in the shadow of the peacock)—I have not experienced this, but I have experienced the fierce sun like the face of the angry Chandi. If I were sitting alone by the stairs of the home in the afternoon, if the water of the well had fallen on the road, if a cow were sitting asleep with her eyes closed and a crow like a vile creature be bothering her by beating her! If one or two dogs were to be sleeping behind the cot laid in the courtyard of Kashi Bua in front and I sitting at the door eating a pocketful of *khinni* (obtuse-leaved mimusops) or *jungle-jalebi* (manila tamarind) and experiment to see how far I can throw the seeds kept in my mouth, at that time I would be seeing a tornado-like ghost rising giddily by moving the paper waste out of the way. Raising my eyes, sometimes I used to try to see that fiery ball of sky. As soon as I saw this, I used to remember the workshop of Lallu blacksmith or the shop of Chhagan goldsmith. When the Lallu blacksmith in his workshop took out the heated red-hot ball of iron from the furnace, at that time he used to look almost like this sun and in the same way our Chhagan goldsmith used to pull some piece of gold out of his kiln by tongs, that time he also turned out to be this sun-bright. I used to think that God must have a huge furnace burning in this sky. This ball seems to have come out of that very furnace. God must be sitting somewhere and burning that furnace, right? Otherwise, where would such a strong hot wind with a blaze of fire blow from?

Such moody silence of the afternoon sun would spread throughout the village. Very few creatures like me or like that crow used to have been conscious at that time. That Gordhan Gandhi of ours, that Lalu *paan*-seller and that old woman Kamu who keeps whining when she was awake—all of them used to have become as quiet as the water of earthen-pot on the platform. If there was a swing somewhere, its creak used to seem like hangover..! I don't know why slumber did not knock at my eyes. The eyes used to remain empty, like completely vacant water-urns, and keep awaking. I used to spread pillow and sack. Used to tie a dhoti or *saree*-sheet all around after soaking them in water. Used to tie father's red turban after making it wet. Still, there were something left, then I used to blow the fan on the body from the front...! But that foe sleep used always to keep a sacred distance of nine yards from me, it did not have the generosity to reduce it even by an iota. Eventually, being tired I used to camp at the door. I used to watch the dusty environment of the road flying like oil without hair flying on the head, it was as if my entire village had taken shape in the mouth of that yawning Krishna on a summer afternoon. The lonely flute, the dry Yamuna, the dilapidated *kadamb* (bur-flower tree), the empty milk-pot, the desolate Madhuvan and the death-ruminating cow as described by Priyakant*. Along with my mind, everything around me also felt heavy. A deep feeling of sadness arises for others and for myself. What should I do? Bringing the charcoal from the stove, I used to draw crooked drawings on the stone of the door. I used to draw improper lines. Used to play the game all alone. If I got tired of this, I used to start practicing my uneducated skill in clay-art by taking mortar from the pile kept in the corner of the porch, and taking the water. Used to make different types of toys from clay. I used to try to make effigy also out of it. Once, I brought black soil from the pond and tried for hours to make Shrinathji out of it. And there was remarkable success too; but toys made of such clay used to be cracked when dried—this was a *yaksh-prashn* (the question, which is too difficult to solve) for me. Later—even after becoming a 'mature' teacher of 'Garvi' Gujarati language—I have still not given up this hobby of mine. Even today, whenever there is time and soil, I like to dance with my fingers in a creative manner. Just five-seven years ago, due to lack of clay, I had tried to make statues of Buddha and Krishna from the pebbles of *daudkhani* wheat, but was not successful, because the pebbles were actually erosion or mud and its structure was not like the potter's black-clay. By the way, I should clarify here that till the time I was writing this, I have no formal knowledge of clay-art, and the glory of whatever I used to do was nothing more than a game. However, many times a good shape could also be formed out of it. Once, a beautiful statue of a dancer was made from clay, but for some reason my father got angry at me, it was broken due to having been thrown by him and

* Priyakant Maniar—a Gujarati poet

at that time such feeling arose within me that was felt by the people when Mahmud Ghaznavi broke the statue of Somnath. Well, I was the one who gave him a solid reason to get angry.

I don't know why, but I am very interested in the faces of men and their speech. Even when I am burdened with a lot of work, I sit in the veranda of my home with a cold heart and keep looking—just keep looking—at the people coming and going. There is no mention of boredom. Time would just slide by with slow, sweet waves. Raghuveer Choudhary—being my true friend, sometimes used to sarcastically interrogate me about the wastage of time. He used to say, "You are not at all conscious about time." Then I used to remember that verse: *'Ajaramaravat prajno vidyamartham cha chintayet...'* (considering that old age and death will never come, an enlightened person should think about acquiring knowledge and wealth...). Instead of knowledge and wealth, I look at this entire creation, at the *leela—srishtim leelam cha 'darsayet',* this is my metric-line; however, to move on such metric-line, one has certainly to be *'pragy'* (enlightened one), then in case of becoming so, no abstinence or irritation even of an iota is there to my consciousness.

But the main thing is about that rural afternoon of mine, when I would get tired of spending the afternoon sitting alone at the door, I used to go straight to the well in my enclosure—to take refuge of Lord Varun (the deity of water). With rope and pitcher! Just as a living being gives up *'jirnani vasansi'* (old clothes), in the same way, with more enthusiasm than Siddhartha, I after removing all the clothes without any attachment used to pour water on my body by drawing it from the well. Twenty-twenty-five pitchers would be an under-statement. Many times, if the playmates were met, we could leave behind even the chariot-race of the Vedic era over a small well, with such thrill there used to be a competition to draw the water-filled pitchers. There used to be a test as to who could pull out the most pitchers from the well and pour them on his body. Sometimes the well would become so shallow that its bottom used to become visible. We would have had to end our water-sport early, unobtainable even for gods, out of fear. Sometime in the afternoon, some elderly persons' sleep would have been broken by our joyous screams. They used to abuse like heat waves. They used to come out running with their hands raised, and we—leaving our pitcher-rope in a helpless state at the edge of the well, taking the clothes and other belongings in our hands, dripping water from our naked bodies—used to have to run with all our might into the enclosure. After reaching some safe place, taking a breath and drying the body, we used to wear those clothes. And after this, when the feeling of safety becomes stronger, we used to start worrying about the baseless pitcher-rope lying on the edge of the well and after keeping those in a suitable place, we used to become worry-free like a affectionate father who has married his daughter at a suitable place.

A delightful programme on hot summer afternoon used to take place in the farms around the village, while roaming around with animals, and plucking down and eating *khinni, jungle-jalebi,* mango, etc. I would open the bamboo row used in home for drying clothes in such a way that the sleeping people of the home do not wake up. Along with this, with the help of rags, twine, etc., I used to make thin-rod of umbrella wire. There would have been a stick for the *gilli,* I would have taken that along and slowly moved out of the home. We used to roam on the ridges of the farms. Used to pluck down *khinni* with lumps, stones, etc. Used to take down *jungle-jaleb*i from a thin rod. If there was a mango tree somewhere and its caretaker was moving here and there, we used also to sift through that Jesus-like mango by pelting it with stones. I would bring salt and pepper in a sac from home and with it our forest-wandering group used to have sit safely under the shade of a tree. There used to be a party of *khinni, jungle-jalebi,* mango etc. If the bull had been without a leather jacket, we used to have drawn water by pulling that. There used to be a crackling sound of the leather jacket. Such a voice, in which some hidden sweet smooth heartbeat of the green earth's heart would also have been mingled. We used to drink coconut-like sweet water palm-cup after palm-cup. If we got a chance, we used to take bath either with or without clothes, and after getting refreshed, used to distribute whatever leftover items remained—*khinni, jungle-jalebi,* mango etc. Being the owner of the thin-rod, I would get two shares and everyone else should get one each. But I did not know how to throw stones, my work was only to pick up the fallen mangoes, *khinni*, etc., hence, keeping in mind my humble efficiency, my share would have been reduced a little; as a result, one and a half share used to be offered to me, but that too was no less. All pockets of shorts and shirt used to be filled well with *jungle-jalebi*, etc. If there was any left, I used to bring it home having kept it in my shirt used like a bag. Everyone at home would have been angry because I had opened the bamboo row and taken it away; but as soon as I stepped into the door, I used to say loudly to my mother, "Mother, I have brought *khinni* and *jungle-jalebi* for Thakurji." Mother's angry face used to become cheerful. She would ask, "You haven't tasted Thakurji's dry fruits, right?" And I used to lie outright and say, "No, no, first you take it out of these for Thakurji, then I will take it." Just as an earning son who brings a bag full of gems from abroad and keep it at his mother's feet, I used to keep *khinni, jungle-jalebi*, etc., at my mother's feet. I used also to make a request to Thakurji in my mind that, "If you have tasted Shabari's plum, then eat this too; and do not feel bad for telling a lie." Then how many times would I have brought *palash* for Thakurji. At home, mother and sister used to make leaf-cups at the rate of hundred. Sometimes, without saying anything, I used to bring a small bundle of leaves for them in excitement and then the joy of my mother's face used as if to bow down even the *palash* leaves; but unfortunately, at that age, I was rarely able to think of any work that would be useful to my family-members.

We used also to plan to spend the long summer afternoons in some cool place. Sometimes, without the family-members knowing, we would go to the pond and lie there like a crocodile. I couldn't swim, so I had to essentially stay near the pier. Some courageous friends used to swim ahead like a turtle, reach the lotus and even tempt someone like me to come to that side. But the fear of drowning in deep water would stop me. Many times, our group used to find a dense bush, clear a place of branches and leaves, collect water and spend three-four hours of the afternoon eating and drinking comfortably. During this time, vegetarian and non-vegetarian jokes and stories were told; 'mimicry' used to be taken place there. Many of us used exactly to mimic the way my father would perform *kirtan*. I used to feel shy, but I couldn't speak anything. Sometimes I felt like doing 'mimicry'; but I used to feel very perturbed, my feelings remained only in my mind. Even today, I have not been able to get out of such a perturbed circumstance as per my wish. Many colours flow in my mind and yet, due to Hamlet-like thinking, I cannot extract even a single colour from within. So, while I have lost a lot, I have also saved a lot from going wrong.

The taste of a clear summer night is different. Sleeping

in a bed in the shed or on the terrace. Like looking at the moon using a butter-filled milk-pot or a pitcher filled with cold water, trying to identify the flowers of the stars and constellations like the jasmine flower on the sky vine and their relationship with them, sometimes in case a white cloud is suddenly seen, then trying to understand its shape, keeping taking out the thread of its pace, sometimes a sweet intoxicating breeze would come filtering through the mango-grove or neem trees, making the soil of the body smell fragrant by drinking it with every breath. Its taste itself was unique.

Then the memories of various fairy-tales or magical stories that I had read would also awaken with a tinkling sound, as if the chandeliers and sheer chandeliers used to twinkle together in the bright sky. It used to seem as if a magic carpet would come flying from some direction. Perhaps that prince's horse will come flying from that direction. Maybe someday a golden-haired princess will come this way and if she comes, can I live without welcoming her? I would get lost in sweet and serious thoughts about how I would welcome the princess if she came and would slip from the path of sleep into the strange streets of dreams. That world was even more magical. Carts after the carts will be filled with the talks of it, but today those carts are not to be left here, nor are those to be unloaded.

Today I stop here–in front of the heat of my village. It is a different matter about urban heat and then it is an even different thing about the perennial heat inside. Even though the furnace is raging inside, you have to keep your face smiling so that the photographer's plate does not get spoiled like Sundaram's mother. Even if a storm arises within, a mirage of humour has to appear on the lips. The inner bottom has burst like a pond without water and yet one has to exclaim, "Look, the beautiful king of seasons has come." Good man, tolerating the inner heat and knowing its secret is not the work of timid people. There are only a few aqua experts who know this secret. The rest all are ordinary people who love sherbet and sweets. How they will know the splendour and sharpness that exist within me!

□

16

Water also has an addiction. There is a flavour of primitiveness in it. Those who know they know this, those who experience it also experience it. Cloud has been my friend since childhood but I met cloud-messenger late. After Gauri left in adolescence! And since I met that, it feels as if I have an old relationship from many lives ago. When the lunar month of Ashadh would come, the emotional rhythm of *'Ashadsya pratham divase'* (the first day of Ashadh) would engulf me. Somewhere in some Alka *(Alkapuri—the abode of Kuber, the demigod of wealth),* that Gauri carved out of lightning and clouds—standing at the skylight of a seven-storey chateau—uses to be visible waiting for me. Wherever her clear vision speckled with pearls used to pause, it would as though create a heap of fragrant night-jasmines. Even the camphor in Gauri's mind used to seem to be fragrant in the sweet fragrance of the water-soaked earth. Gauri used to keep swinging on the pavilion of my mind like a creeper. of *juhi*-flowers. Buds of tears of love used to keep falling from her eyes. Her touch used to give a tinkling sound of some sitar in me. Everything used to seem so sweet and lovely-and-alluring to me...! But I will not tell you the exact date when such an experience started happening.

If someone asked me to choose only two senses to enjoy the rainy season, I would prefer the sense-of-smell and the sense-of-touch first. While catching the nectar-torrent of rain, I would feel as if I was touching the distant, untouched sky with my palm. I felt so fortunate that the water-drops had come together even with those stars in the sky. How many times I would even colourfully imagine reaching Gauri through the drawn bow of the rainbow. During my teenage years, after becoming friends with the cloud-messenger, many times I would try to find and catch the bodiless Gauri among some black and white clouds. Many times, by reciting the poetic lines of Kalidas, I would try to reach Gauri's mental world through the wind-deity and cloud; but Gauri, like a goddess *prakashmurti* (idol of lights), would appear far away even if she was nearby. Gauri—wearing white clothes with open braid—appeared to me, shining steadily like the pure light of a waiting-lamp; but I could not hold her fingers as soft as tender-leaves. Looking at the far-distant moon again and again I would feel the waves of my consciousness like the ocean crashing against the rocks. The shore is not acceptable and also, no violation of the shore used to take place.

Sometimes, in the sweet night of the midnight, when the moon is covered under the cover of dark clouds in the sky on the full-moon night of Ashadh or Shravan, when the trees and vines are dripping the pearls of sweet memories of the remaining rain, then Gauri—being incarnated in the form of a well-shaped idol of intoxicating beauty-essence of the clouds—would be coming for commingling me carrying a golden lamp-plate in her lotus-hands. If it is not so, why would she come closer to me, I thought. Why would all the silver-bells of my inner palace ring simultaneously at the mere thought of Gauri's commingle? Why would my five elements—earth, water, fire, air and sky—come together and rejoice, giving the unique taste of *panchamrit* (an ambrosia made of five ingredients)?

Many times, such happening is being taken place to me as if someone has planted the graft of Gauri's consciousness in my consciousness and is trying to grow it by uniting it with some ever-renewed sap of divine-oneness through the skill of magical water—and that too, in this creative season of rains. Gauri's extraterrestrial presence appears to me in many forms this year: sometimes, Gauri appears like a scarlet-line of beauty in the light of the green leaves of a newly-bathed jasmine. Sometimes, I feel the bent posture of her vision in the graceful bow of the rainbow. Sometimes, in the stream of a waterfall, I feel the tinkling sound of Gauri's anklets flowing. On appearing in front of my inner eyes, to my inner ears, Gauri becomes titillated in my entire consciousness like the grass is blossomed up from the soil. Rain comes and Gauri's remembrance bounces on both edges. Her absence fills within me, she overflows from my eyes.

Along with the memory of rain, the boat—that of the paper boat—also comes to mind. By collecting different types of colourful, small and big papers, we used to make boats out of those and float those wherever there the rain-water was logged or flowing. Sometimes, Gauri would also join in floating the boat in this manner. These were paper boats; Gauri and I were not going to be able to sit in them. Despite that, there was no doubt, we would have gently seated *dhundhachi* and *chiya* in the boat as our representatives. If *dhundhachi* belonged to Gauri, then *chiya* was mine. We used to keep staring at the boat floating in the water. Sometimes it would wobble sideways, sometimes it would stop in the middle, and sometimes it would capsize on its own without being able to control itself, then we used to be careful as much as possible to save *dhundhachi* and *chiya* from getting swept away in the water or getting lost; but personally speaking, my alertness turned out to be half-baked. *Dhundhachi* remained, but Gauri was gone...! By the way, I strongly believe that my *chiya* would still be shining clean in the strong determined fist of Gauri's delicate hand.

The grandest event during the rainy season was water-sports and sky-bathing. The first rains were about to come, birds used to start bathing in the dust and we would start feeling severe itching all over our body due to prickly-rashes. Like every time I used to tell my mother; this time, I will have to take bath regularly during the rainy season, only then the prickly-rashes would reduce and disappear. Mother too, seeing my pain from scratching, used to say 'yes' with compassion. In this way, with prior security, I used to observe the series of clouds appearing in the sky again and again. When would the flocks of clouds come here and when I would be getting drenched in its waters with all my might.

Whenever it rained, we would all—being naked—jump like frogs from the door and go to the locality, apply dust on our bodies and then stand under the terracotta-made roof-tiles of the houses and wash it. Just as there are many 'points' on Abu, similarly certain 'points' for our bathing were fixed in advance. The programme of when to go to the temple and when to go to that inn was also planned. Sometimes we would take bath under the tile and would simultaneously keep competition about urine-flow. There was no shame, no calculation of good or bad. Letting the water fall on the bare head, back, chest, filling the water in palm-cup and gulping it down; drinking water directly from the sky with mouth wide open, pouring water on others and getting wet with water through others, gargling water and spraying it in the air like a fountain with water in the mouth, falling asleep flat on the back in the flow of water—in these many ways continuing the interesting business of connecting the body and mind with water in a playful way—this was our only self-duty at that time.

While we were playing with water, we would also be playing other new games. When the rains come, earthworms used also to come out. We used to keep them in a box and bring the flute (where would the beans be from) and play the game of juggler. The earthworm was our virtuous snake grandfather. Sometimes we would divert and fill the water in various ways by building a pond, well or canal by digging a pit or by digging a pit. Many times, some insects would sit on empty match boxes or sticks and start floating in this water. How many times we used to make a Shivling of mud and perform the ritual of reciting *shivstotra* (a hymn devoted to Shiv) in front of it. Sometimes we used to make a lump of black-clay on a plate, insert two eyes made of cowry and take out the procession of Mehul-Meghraja and would roam around the entire locality with Meghraja placed on the head.

When the rain stopped, the game of 'Kochmani'* used to be played. Our group would roam from one end of the village to the other carrying a pointed bar for this game. Many times, I used to lose in this game and hence I would have to serve for the chance of leg-trick and if my feet touched the ground while taking the leg-trick, I used to get a punch as well. I could bear the punch, but could not bear to leave the game.

But when this rain continued continuously for five-seven days, we used to become very restless. The walls used to be completely wet and there would be a foul smell. The wind used to be dampened. Muddy milk-like sharpness. The same tapping sound from the terracotta-made roof-tiles, like a government typewriter. It used to seem that if we stayed at home, yeast would rise inside us.

---

* A game played with a thin bar in wet soil.

The eyes again and again would peek out of the nest-like home, and come back from the rainy cold. Ant-houses used to start emerging at various places in the whitewash of the home. Flocks of flies used to keep buzzing here-and-there. Flies would also stick to the bars of the swing. One cannot even sit (or sleep) properly due to jealous flies. Sometimes I would think that if I had a cannon nearby, I could fire one or two shells and scatter the clouds in the sky. Even a cannon ball would be dampened in this air. Ultimately, as there would be dampened sticks lying in the matchbox, in this way I used to be lying everywhere on the sack in the home, but how would I get peace? At last, I used to wake up, pick up coal from somewhere, and draw criss-crossing railway tracks on the earthen-floor. I used to drive the train using an empty matchbox or blowing authoritatively the whistle given to me by my father after a pilgrimage. When Gauri was alive, she too used to be involved in driving the train...*dhook, bhook, jhook, jhook*—the train used to move sounding like this. The train used to bring the desired guests and stop at the desired station. It would also bring the afternoon snack, and Gauri and I used to eat it together. Sometimes we felt like calling God in this gathering of both of us, that is why our train used to go to God sounding like *chhuk...bhuk...chhuk...bhuk*. It used to return safely carrying Him. We would let God play with us for as long as we wanted and then when we used to get tired of playing with Him or become bored, we used to give Him a ticket and send Him back. Many times, this God would stubbornly refuse to leave both of us, but could we tolerate such a breach of discipline? We used to breathe only after sending Him forcibly to His abode like parcels by adding two engines instead of one. But then Gauri was gone, similarly Girdhari was also gone and along with them, my childhood too. At this time, after the strong flow of water has ended, only the remains of the deserted ravines created by it have remained in this soil. There are, undoubtedly, a few trees here and there on the shore—those too with fallen leaves. Those poor trees don't have enough shade to cool down the heat or humidity inside me. Today, the days of water's fish have come to swim in mirage. Okay brother!

I used to count the rainy days from festivals. This is *Ashadh Vat-amavasya,* this *Rakhi-poonam,* this *Shitala-satam,* this *Janmashtami,* this *Dussehra,* this *Sharad-poonam*—like this. Cold food of *Shitala-satam, barfi* and *panjiri* of *Janmashtami, kheer* and *laddus* during *Shraddha* days, milk-and-flattened-rice of *Sharad-poonam*. Thus, in many ways, this rainy season of mine used to become a delicious dessert.

During the rains, I often enjoyed crossing the streams on the way, digging in the green farms and taking a walk by the pond. Used to go to an English school from one village to another. Where would I have the lordliness of possessing an umbrella or raincoat from? It was enough that the books for reading, wrapped in waxed-paper, would be protected from the rain. Many times, I used to get wet in the rain and spend the whole day in school in those wet clothes. Used to come back home in the evening. Because of being caught by cold, I used to suffer from catarrh again and again. At home, when I sneezed and felt my head heavy, mother used to cook hot porridge by adding dry-ginger and long-pepper-root to millet flour and at that time, I would feel such warmth and freshness of mother's love in the porridge that I used to feel by heart, which is strongly marked even today.

The carousel in our Vaishnav-temple was very magnificent during the rainy season. Mango-leaves, flowers, vegetables, zari-silk, etc.—thus in various ways we used to adorn this carousel. Father had meticulous supervision and instructions regarding this. The carousel used to be adorned in about five-seven hours. The fun of adorning it was also unique. Many times, the elders would go back-and-forth a bit after delegating some of the primary work of adorning the carousel to the younger ones like us; and then one of us, a naughty boy, used to sit on the carousel in place of Thakurji himself and hit five or ten sways. We all used to have watched this act of courage, but why did we use even to grumble in low tone? I too would have wanted to swing on the carousel like him, but the thought of sin and my father's wrath used to have suppressed this desire of mine. This suppressed desire used to explode while swinging on the swing at home. I used to sit on the swing with the flute on my lips in the manner of Krishna, and if Gauri came in such a situation, she would get me swung as much as I wished for.

How many times did we use also to play the game of Thakurji's carousel at home. The brass Lalji was made to sit in the swing, but he used to fall again and again. We, Gauri and I, used to have felt bad due to this. Once Gauri got angry and said—"I don't understand if you sit like this. If you had just fallen on the ground having turned around, your temples would have turned red." But Lalji was of real mettle. He didn't listen to what Gauri said. Ultimately, both of us unanimously declared Him unfit for this game and demoted Him.

Today Gauri is not there, nor that Lalji of ours, then where is that Chandrakant? Where is even that rain today? Today there are feet, but not those delicate steps, which do dance up by the art of 'omission-mark' *(kak-pad)* or the art of peacock in the rain-soaked soil.

□

17

I talked about the intoxication of water, but did not talk about the 'sparsely-woven warmth of water'. I didn't do so because I don't feel like upsetting anyone by unnecessarily involving them in such a thing. Some things are meant to be understood and some to be tolerated, not meant to be conveyed to everyone. There are innumerable forms of water, but the water that flows squeezing our entire being is unique. There is some water which neither warms, drowns nor calms. There is fire in that water or that water is a form of fire itself.

But why should I get trapped in a vortex of water like this? Where did I get trapped in the tricks of a picture leaving the foot-gaits of the child-and-teenager? Cleaning my eyes, removing the curtain of water I should look inside. Inside there is not only the light of the moon and the sun, but also the abstinent-diet like light of the lamp flickering in the niche in Manchhi aunt's home; and along with it there is also the rotten-local-autonomy like sterile light of *panchayat's* lantern repeatedly infuriating and spewing black smoke. In it, there is the light of the terrible burning-infuriating torch of our Magna barber, and along with it there is also the benevolent light of *'petromax'* hanging upside down on the pillar in Mahadevwale Chowk. The garlands—made with the delicate spheres carved out of rosewood, besides the *zari*-and-golden-embroideries and the flowers—for covering the groom's head in sedan, and the ride, and the earth (although it is masculine gender, but we use to use as feminine gender only. What will you do, dear grammarian?) that adopts different guises, and that Chandu coppersmith of ours who in the afternoon used to weld and polish the brass utensils, but pump the *petromax* during Ramlila in the form of 'darling electricity'—the unique and colourful creation of all these gets revealed in the light of such a *petromax*. The new-novel disorders visible on our faces reflected on the gleaming mansion of *petromax* have also been beautifully kneaded in it. Now when I am writing this, I find the light of *petromax* more exciting and exhilarating than the light of the sun and moon. It comes to my mind, I should ask the Almighty that apart from this *petromax,* all the lights—except the light of eyes—O God! Get those wrapped up! Get those be gone.

In the light of this *petromax,* I start gliding with much pace. Descending the stairs of years, towards the inn with that typical Ramji temple. Here Gopal, the polymorph, is being seen. Although he is fifty-five-sixty years old, but his personality is impressive glinting with liveliness. Every year, he certainly used to come to our village at least once without fail. Used to stay for twenty-thirty days. Used to adopt new-novel disguises. On days when the polymorph Gopal used to come out in the guise of monkey, he would take a handful or two of whatever edible-items were kept on the cot in the courtyard and put that in his mouth. Whenever the polymorph Gopal used to come out in the guise of Saraswati, at that time all of us schoolboys would devoutly put a penny or two in his plate and pray in our hearts for good studies. Once this polymorph had guised as a police inspector and around 3-4 pm, scolding seven-eight shopkeepers he along with the police raided at the moneylenders and even wrote down *panchnama* (record of witness-testimony). A bribe of twenty-five-fifty rupees was also taken from everyone and snacks were taken separately. In the evening, when the polymorph Gopal started cheerfully giving back the money taken from the places where he had raided, then the scandal broke—everyone realised the reality. We, the children and teenagers, kept a keen eye on the day-long programme of this polymorph, but in this disguise, we too couldn't guess the reality. We had received news that today Gopal was to adopt a guise of a Marwari *seth,* but his guise turned out to be a police inspector. Due to this polymorph person, some important games of polymorph were included in our games. The cap made from the bag, father's spectacles, the toy-revolver for bursting cracker-ribbon, elder brother's old leather belt—taking all these, there is a firm memory of adopting the guise as Subhash Babu.

Just as the nights in our village remained tasteful due to the polymorph, similarly, due to Ramlila, Kathaparayan, etc., the Ramlila people have come to the village, this was a very important news for us, it was as if the country had got independence. After having my meal quickly, I used to reach the place where Ramlila was to take place, and find a good place there. After this, I used to definitely see the grand preparations they made for Ramlila despite their refusal or threats; and used to spread its story among our other friends: Chandu coppersmith wears a blouse, puts round pieces of cloth to show the chest in the blouse, now he is wearing *saree,* now he is doing make-up on his face—thus my running-commentary used to be continued. On the other hand, I used to be ready to help in every way for Ramlila. 'Hey, hey, boy, please bring the table.' Immediately, I used to run to nearby houses to bring the table. Had anyone asked for water, it would have been available. If asked to keep harmonium and *tabla,* I used to be ready (and I also used to lovingly give a couple of slaps on the *tabla*.) I was only anxious about when the Ramlila would begin. Even in the Ramlila, I liked Bajrangbali and Narad more than Ram. If a clown had appeared in that too, then *aa ha ha*...! I used to wonder why these people keep only one clown in Ramlila? Four or five were needed. I used to have enjoyed the joy and fun of the love between the clown and Gauri to my heart's content.

The unpleasant thing for me in this Ramlila was the *aarti*. There was no fixed recital of *aarti* in the Ramlila and unless the donation-of-cereals for the next day was confirmed to them, the Ramlila left incomplete was not carried forward. I used to be very bored with their slowness. I felt that if I had been the Thakur of the village, I used to have given the money and donation of cereals to the people of Ramlila for the whole month's *aarti* in just one go with no hesitation; but where were those days that...

This Ramlila used to continue till one-two o'clock in the night. I was allowed by home to attend Ramlila only till eleven o'clock. But somehow, I could not sleep and did not feel like leaving Ramlila midway. Once, the play of Sita Swayamvar was being staged. Sitaji was standing in front of a broken wooden chair—throne—holding a garland. Ramchandraji was preparing to break the Shivdhanush by pulling its string. All the viewers seemed to be engrossed as if in meditation. They had oneness with the scene in their sight and mind; and just then, as if the Ramlila's curtain of colourful dramatic ambience was getting be torn sounding *cha...r...r...r...*, a harsh voice came up with the father's cane sounding *thak-thak*—"Chandrakant...!" I was shocked as if a hot ember had touched my ear. In the meantime, someone from the viewers, who was distracted, said, "This uncle is also strange. The play was perfectly going on, but just then he made all the fun ruined." That night, while lying down on the bed at home I had flawlessly woken up whole the night to enjoy Ramlila even by getting my ears run.

It is worth knowing the story of Chandu coppersmith voluntarily joining the 'Ramlila' organized in the village. Son without parents. Was poor. Somehow, he learnt the work of a coppersmith. Meanwhile he found a loose woman. They got married, but could not live together for long. Whatever belongings were in the house, she collected everything and went away. Chandu was left alone, hence he got addicted to alcohol and became a pauper. Still this addiction has not been cured. If he had earned two-five rupees by working as a coppersmith, half of it would have been spent on alcohol. He used to spend the whole day welding utensils and polishing, neither having any special conversation or joking with anyone, but when night fell, he would apply powder on his face, wear *lehenga-chunari* and participate in the Ramlila plays, then that Chandu looked completely different. There the clown used to call him 'Vataki'. What a reputation he had there! What a lustre his speech had, as well. I used to think: in which storehouse of heart had Chandu stored all these jewels and ornaments? In which safe deposit vault had he preserved all these? So many colours and so many different types of beautiful wars were hidden in his inner sky. After seeing Chandu's skill in the Ramlila, Chandu was not mere coppersmith for me, but had become more important. With this intention so that Chandu could get jobs, we boys after going home would inform our mother about the utensils with holes and rust and insist on getting those repaired and when the mother would approve, taking the utensils, we would immediately be present in Chandu's service. Sometimes when Chandu permitted, we used also to turn on the fan of his furnace.

My father had some feeling of indifference towards this Ramlila. The reason for this was that Ramchandra was *maryada-purushottam* (the most dignified among men) and my father was a *pushtimargi*—hence for him, Sri Krishna was *poorn-purushottam* (the complete supreme One). When a troupe of Raasdharis used to come to perform the *leela* of Sri-Krishna, without missing a single day he would watch the performance of that troupe of Raasdharis. The way they used to sing and speak dialogues in the Braj language, my father used to keep those in his mind with full interest and taste and sometimes would recite two or five dialogues or lines also from memory as samples. We also had complete freedom to watch Raaslila. When Sri Krishna and Radha came to the Raaslila, my mother and sister etc., used to obtain the dust of their feet by touching their feet, and also put money as per their capacity.

The way the polymorph, Ramlila people used to come regularly to our village, the Bhavai people too would come. They used to stay in the village. I was not allowed to watch Bhavai (folk-drama of Gujarat). When father used to go to another village for service-related work, I, disregarding mother would set out to see Bhawai, without paying the slightest attention to the prohibition and order issued by her. There was a lot of abuses in Bhavai, but everyone was the child of *aadi-shakti* (the primal power) Jagdamba (Durga). It was believed that the generous and kind Mother would forgive their mischievousness. Many obscene things about Bhavai come to mind while writing here, but it is not necessary to mention those in this writing.

Today, when I remember the Ramlila-people, Raaslila-people and Bhavai-people, then it seems that the power, the immense but raw gold of emotion-material and language that I got to see in Bhavai is the exclusive. The way these Bhavai people imitated the eighteen classes, the ruthless visitation of worldliness they used to get made and the several tricks they used to get people laugh—the talk of those is unique. The *rekhta* (verses) that were recited in Bhavai, the dance of *tata...tha...thei...thei* used to be performed accompanied by blowing the horn—those used to make the mind drenched in rhythm-and-sound, those do so even today.

Then, sometimes Bhattji Puranik who would recite tales or *saint-bhajnik* who would sing *bhajan-kirtan* used also to come to the village. Specially, Bhattji, who recited almost the entire Mahabharata for a month, is being remembered by me at this time. Huge body and sweet tongue. As soon as he arrived, he brought the entire village under control. During one month's stay in the village, not a single day was spent without a solid meal of juicy *laddus*. He would have kept a harmonium with him that he could play with his feet. For accompaniment, a *tabla*-player would be found in the village, he used to play the harmonium with both hands and recite the tale. His style of recitation was very dramatic, and the taste of all the emotions—love and courage, humour and sorrow, anger and fear—used to be provided by him thoroughly. Even the avid *bhagwat*-lovers like my father were attracted to Bhattji. The day Bhattji completed the tale, the procession of his book was taken out in the village with great fanfare. When Bhattji left, the entire village cried. Everyone felt his absence. Bhattji had promised to come next year, but never came again.

Just as my consciousness used to be stimulated by the beat of the Bhavai, similarly it used also to be jumped and infuriated by the piercing and hypnotic sound of the drum. A person possessed by a ghost would be taken to Bhathi Khatriji's temple at night. The incense used to be lit, the coconut used to be broken, our Veer Singh Ojha would slowly start trembling, shaking and rotating. On him, Bhathiji used to have come himself. Veer Singh now stands up. Fixing a lemon on the tip in red-sacred-thread hand, he swings a vermilion-applied sword, and along with it he delicately shakes a bunch of peacock feathers. *Gulal* flies. Veer Singh Ojha's roar is heard. A verse in praise of Bhathiji is sung along with the drums. The fragrant rose-coloured light of the incense lamp binds the ambience with some indescribable irresistible excitement.

I too get a lot of thrill from this incident. While carrying knife and lancet and playing drums of cans at the home, I too call Bhathiji, and just then someone informs, "Kaka (father) is coming." Immediately, it was as if someone had put a piece of ice in the boiling milk. Everything gets dispersed—becomes quiet. Hushed! Father would look at the knife-and-lancet and say, "Are these things worth for playing with? What if it hits somewhere?" I move away silently from there. The thought occurs in my mind: when will such a unique opportunity come, when this life woven into everything—Ramlila, Raaslila, Bhavai and the guise of polymorph—also takes Patan's embroidered *paton (saree)* like beauteous appearance? Should my life be visible like that Ramlila, Raaslila? Will something like this never happen that I become worth listening to and memorable? I think: I should have made a close friendship with that Gopal polymorph, and that Chandu coppersmith. Now if I get a chance for such friendship, do you think, sir, I will delay even for a moment?

□

18

If this statement—distant drums sound well—is true for the places, then is it not true for life too? Our everyday life seems so pleasant and exciting when we observe it from a distance. Today, after so many years, when I look back, I feel that many things are attracting me with their eyes dancing. These things didn't seem as attractive at that time as these do today. I had to walk from Kanjari to Halol school every day and at that time I found that route as boring as a textbook lesson. Today, it looks elegant like a golden line drawn between the clouds. I don't know whether that dusty path of mine has become urban bitumen or not. For us humans, a bushed thorny trail or a rough-bumpy, trampled, muddy or gravelly path—everything suits as per the situation; but that attractive car needs a smooth-plane road. The poor feet can walk even on narrow stairs, but those tyre-vehicles? Those want beautiful bitumen or asphalt roads.

Don't know why; despite having been tended myself de-pastured on this bitumen even year-after-year, the fascination of the dusty path does not fade away. With the first drops of rain, the hope of green grass shines. One begins to taste the aroma of soil. The fragrance of sweet night spills out in my mind due to raindrops. Just as one gets satisfaction by eating pulses-and-rice with the tips of the fingers, just as one gets satisfaction by drinking water by holding a glass to the lips, the same happens to the soles of the feet. I also feel freshness as soon as I touch the soil. Truly, I have an inner relationship with the soil, I have a deep connection with it.

Be it soil or water, be it wind or light or the boundless sky around, at that time, due to their contact, all the five elements—earth, water, fire, air and sky—start swinging in me. The freshness of greenery begins to spread being irrigated in every pore of mine! The sunlight rising in the window of my home begins awakening some extraordinary freshness of joy by being come down to my blood. The sky, filled with the beauty of the earth, starts waving a gentle image of happiness in my mind sliding over the delicate chin of a village girl. Truly, there is some element in this soil, in this air, in this water, which by opening up the reserves within me provides necessity to the creation existed there to flourish easily. In these trees, in these waterfalls, in these mountains and greenery, in the brightness of these stars and the glimpse of lightning, there is marked a strong posture of my astonishment, my pervasiveness, my eternity. I have reached today's ladder by intertwining myself with everyone, weaving everyone into myself. Now, I will go even further...

Anyway, I should say, I probably wouldn't have been able to write the way I write today when I was younger. Today, I relish the sweetness of this to my heart's content through the *paan* of memory; I had experienced it to some extent, and its actualisation to some extent was true at that time. I used not to feel good within the boundary-wall of the home. Sitting at the window, sucking one mango after another in summer, looking at the scenery on the road, doesn't seem boring to me at all; rather, it seemed more interesting. Believe it or not, I used to feel a feeling of openness on the terrace and a glow while walking on the path, but it is certain that at some point, 'some serpent of beauty' had bitten me from somewhere—and the 'serpent of greenery' had already bitten me from somewhere. And that is why, since childhood, I have been feeling that my mind has been crawling in shades of internal and external forms, and has been flaunting-and-coiling with colours.

Today, being a humble poet, when I think about the word, my mind spills up with astonishment and joy. How many words, in so many ways, how many times did they come to me? How many words were sown into my consciousness every day. Continuous sowing. Continuous harvesting. A bird-flock of words swells up in my mind. The flutter of delicate wings and the soft melodious-sound. The specific breed of each word should remain imprinted before the eyes. The clamour of its feet should start jingling metrical-rhythm in the consciousness. Some divine element taking the form of words should wave in the overall consciousness. I am just an instrument. Whirlwinds of the element of sound should be hovering from throat to call. After all these whirlwinds rise up from the depth of the inner most, the transformation of mine into some rhythm-full joy takes place. The horns of that 'Bhavai', the notes of that harmonium, the beats of that *tabla,* and the chimes of that cymbal, the *druming-truming* of that drum and the edged plate, the songs of the plate-instruments of the durbar-fort and the saffron tone of the *bhajan*-groups of the Baraiya-Dharala brothers, the theatrical claps of the pavilion, and the loud intonation of my father's *kirtan*—how much a beautiful embroidered theatrical curtain of Sound—the Almighty *(Naad-Brahm)* intertwining-weaving-relishing-colouring with each other had been achieved to be actualised, and receiving this it is still waving within me. The silence of the words of the lips defeated by bashfulness and the silent outspokenness of the loving speech of the eyes, like a secret waterfall, poignantly springs up in the inner rocks. Today, the lines of the letters in which I try to portray myself, those rising from the paper and growing get hidden being dragged—who knows where—behind the horizon. A number-song like *'ek se aawe aikdo, aikdo ne be minda sau'* (one makes one, and two zeros make one hundred) is used to be sung. In this song, a direction can open out of number to intimacy, the moment the restlessness of opening this direction has started to be understood little by little, since then something has started to be understood.

While committing the alphabet to memory, I would start composing poetry out of it, I understood this only after years of experience and when I understood this, there was no limit to my joy. Oho! Up to which-where place have the roots of my speech spread? The hum of that bird's throat, the noise of that fun, the sound of the bell of that Shiv-temple and the call of *'jagte raho'* (stay awake) from my durbar-fort, the noise of the flour mill of my village and the jingle of the bell around the neck of that bull pulling the plough—all these together keep stimulating a sound-lotus in my navel. The motion-throb of butterfly-wings must have also resonated in it. A feeling of poetic joy runs through every vein of mine. I am not disturbed. Nothing 'mine' to me, no death to me. The milk-pot which easily secretes the essence of the universe is my poetry, it is my true form. The way it is understood today, even though I did not understand it in childhood, but the 'divinatory-play of milk' *(goras-leela)*—I had found that this was an innate miracle of childhood.

There was a forest of many faces shining with freshness around me. Zealous and selfish, penniless and overbearing, cool and playful, compassionate and miserly—the colourful creation-web of various faces, engulfing me too, used to be kept forming all around me. Oho! I used to look at that web the way someone looks at a chessboard. It was fun to see which piece goes where and gets stuck, where it hits, where it becomes defeated and where it wins, where it stops. That fun still leaps up in my inner most in the same way.

There were so many people who inspired me, instructed me, shaped me and guided me. As if the potter-wheel of the entire village, while moving round-and-round, gives my being as per its pleasure. Someone awakened the tears of my eyes and someone wiped those. Someone made me laugh aloud and someone even baked me in the fireplace. As a result of all this, the pier I found was just right. Looking at it and thinking over it from a healthy perspective, I don't see any reason to complain about myself. If I walked, I grazed; if I got something lost, I found something; if I was rubbed, I became solid; if I got lost, I got chance to roam. I feel that I have shown my readiness to properly carry out the adaptability that was needed to me in order to let the world around me be expressed through myself. How much that world used me, of course, is a different matter.

Gijubhai Badheka was not the only person, who drove my cart of life. Many hands have given me the fingers to guide me. Whosever character I had read, he would start walking with me. Once, I became inspired by Shankaracharya's fingers, leaving home I reached the outskirts of the village, but due to my good fortune and Gujarati language and literature, I came back on my own. For the second time I decided to become Subhash Babu, I tried to form *Azad Hind Fauj* in my locality, but unfortunately, I did not know how to lead. (Even today I don't know it!). Then I decided to become Gandhi. To become Gandhiji one needs *khadi*. And father gave a strict prohibition order against it. Poor Gandhi, who could not take advantage of me. At last Rabindranath came into my sight. He was a poet not only by deed, but also by appearance. What attracted me more was his appearance rather than his poetry. I thought I should become like him. And for that reason, I started worshiping the poetry through worshipping the poet. During this time, I also read children's literature, the desire to write some rhymes according to their poetry started creeping in and my work started. The verse that I needed started coming out clearly. Initially rhymes, then winters, summers, rains started coming into poetry and then the love. I remember that the first poem was called *'eva Bapu amar raho'* (May such Bapu remain immortal).

In poetry, my cart started running properly. There wasn't much competition, so there was my sway. Otherwise, I was backward in physical ability, wealth and sports, etc., hence I was considered advanced in reading and writing. The ego nourished. Diaries and notebooks started filling up. In the beginning, there was no criticism and evaluation. There was only superficial comparison. I used to write poetry in my own way and then compare it with the poetic creations of accomplished poets. Used to do pruning etc. Fortunately, the matter of publishing came later. The first poem was published in English in class three (today class seven), in the school's handwritten magazine. Since then, I started meeting the poet within me and through this meeting. Over time, I have brought this *kanvad* of fragrance to you today. Call it a fortunate accident, or call it a coincidence, a transaction, a debt-contract.

This 'debt-contract' is really a wonderful word. To which things it does keep bound—and connect—us with itself and around? How does it bind? Someone resides in the heart with authority, someone resides in memory or imagination, someone being made for you resides in your home throughout the life. What was not yours, that comes to you being made of yours. She/he mixes themselves with your words. What is all this? Whatever it may be—illusion, stupidity, miracle, knowledge, encounter—without this spice there is no taste in my existence. Perhaps today, despite suffering, despite countless experiences of hypocrisy and arrogance, my building is still safe. The residents of this building are also happy and prosperous. They have goblet in their hand—and that too, spilling out. Are there tears, wine, sherbet or nectar? Everything is there, kind! All! Drink just one sip and become drunk in its intoxication—at the home and in the veil, in the verses and in the recollection. If it is not there, nothing is there; if it is there, I possess a lot—possess the words of mine struggling like a fish.

□□□